# BLADE
## OF
# SHADOW

SEVEN SWORDS
BOOK 2

## SARAH K. L. WILSON

PUBLISHED BY SPARKFLIGHT BOOKS, 2022

This is a work of fiction. Similarities to real people, places, or events are entirely coincidental.
BLADE OF SHADOW
First Edition. April 1, 2022
Copyright © 2022 Sarah K. L. Wilson
ISBN : 978-1-990516-24-5
Cover Art by Polar Engine
Written by Sarah K. L. Wilson
Published by Sparkflight Books
www.sarahklwilson.com

For Melissa, who has plumbed
the depths of books with me, and
climbed their heights, and known
the joys of the great and sorrows
of the disappointing yet still stayed
with me in our long quest to learn
these tangled ways of the path of
story.

# Chapter One

For a second time, I find myself facing a door, knowing full and well that behind it is a monster bent on my death.

Of course there is.

Monsters love me. Or at least, they love the idea of my death.

This time, though, I have no Mercy Sword glinting in my hands. They'd offered me a curving cutlass bearing the curved etching of a swimming fish. Its forked tail spans the grip and circles the pommel. I'd taken it boldly and without comment.

I'm determined to stay silent so no one hears the squeak in my voice that I know will be there.

"She's really good – a true monster hunter," the Duke says in a whisper. He's close enough behind me that I can hear his whisper but not close enough that he can't leg it out of the ship's hold and back up to the deck if he needs to. He's remarkably adept at keeping his lines of retreat clear.

I can't help it. I love that about him.

The door shudders. This most recent blow makes a creaking sound that works its way down my spine. Everyone behind me flinches so hard I can hear it without turning around. A board

someone nailed across it the door splits with a crack loud enough
to make us all shiver, a single nail popping from its place to
tumble to the deck and roll away.

I hear a nervous chuckle at that.

I check my grip, raising the blade, chin up. If I'm going to
die – especially in front of an audience – I want to try for a little
dignity.

It's different than last time, Ilsaletta, I tell myself. You aren't
the victim cowering in the closet. You're the one *outside* the
door. But if you don't do this, then you lose your chance to stop
Jendaya.

Even with my own words in my head, I'd better do it quickly
or risk my gorge rising in front of all these witnesses. I can feel it
creeping up my throat. I'm not ready to be the one on the attack.

"She's just a little thing," the ship's captain whispers, doubt
heavy as his own ship's anchor. "Look at those arms – skinny.
Pretty enough, I'd say, but she's no brawler and no trained
warrior, neither. I spotted no callouses on her pretty hands as you
two were pulled aboard. Doesn't even have her sea legs. And that's
no monster hunter's dress. Minor nobility would be my guess.
Daughter of a count, mayhap."

I fight back the hysterical laugh threatening to tear from my
throat. It's a princess's dress, stolen by me just last night, and if
the princess ever sees me in it, she'll torture me, kill me, bury me,
and then dig me up and do it again. I pull my father's ship's coat
tighter around the flimsy dress. I feel worse than naked in this
lie of a dress with everyone watching me. Nothing I do seems to
warm me. I can't stay standing like this. I need to act before they
all know what a fraud I am.

Come on, Ilsaletta. Open the door, I tell myself, but I sound weak even in my own head.

"I swear to you, she can fight them," Stekkan says fervently. He should be fervent. We won't find another ship willing to bring us aboard – not with Saltfast in ruins behind us and the princess's soldiers surely on our tails. It's only luck that brought us aboard this one. It's our one chance – even if I don't like it. "I saw her fight a dozen grown men yesterday, and she won."

"These are no men," the captain says. "Gods of sea and sky have mercy, but these things are no human creatures. Not anymore. They'll rip her to shreds and then feast on her butterfly carcass."

I agree.

My shadow shifts unnaturally before me and Vargaard's shadow form seems to flicker as it coalesced.

*"Ready?"* he asks me, quick and sure as always.

Ready? Ha! I will never be ready for these moments.

*"We don't have to do this."*

But we do. It's this or die on the beach.

We'd spotted the ship only moments after Stekkan had awoken on the sand. She was drifting, sails down. We'd rowed out to her, surprising the crew. And no wonder. They'd just finished barring three of their number and one stranger in the hold. Sick. Worse than sick. Possessed. Just the sight of us had terrified them.

"You must leave," they'd said with wide eyes. "No strangers. Not after what happened last night."

Until the Duke offered me up like a prize dog in a dog fight. I'd never seen a dog fight, but I'd read about them. I was pretty certain the dogs felt like I did. Cornered. Desperate.

That was five minutes ago. Just long enough to get me a cutlass. Just long enough for me to stand here in this frothy dress – a dress only a princess would ever wear. Who else would stitch a faux breastplate onto the bodice? – and listen as the corricles smashed and shattered anything that had been in this part of the hold before they were locked in.

I hadn't slept last night – would that make my hands shake?

*Probably. Let me do the fighting. Just keep your blade up high so they don't land a strike on you if they get past me.*

The bar across the door splinters again, enough that it is easy for me to wrench the remains of it free with a trembling hand. I can barely hear Stekkan speaking through the pulse of my blood in my ears, but I know the sailors are hanging on his every word.

"She rescued me the night before yesterday. Tore through a band of them like a hawk through a flock of songbirds."

"She looks noble," the first mate opines. "Has a set to her jaw a bit like old man Saltfast's, if you know my meaning."

"The Admiral," the captain agrees.

This conversation isn't going anywhere I want it to go. Best to end it fast.

I rip the last chunk of shattered wood away from what used to be a bar across the door.

*"Steady now,"* Vargaard says. *"Open the door quickly and then step smartly to the left."*

The wood has that shiny smooth feel of wood that's seen a lot of use. I try to hold onto that feeling so I don't have to think about how the creatures behind it are hitting the door so hard and fast they might as well be deck drummers on His Majesty's ships. About how I'm not sure I know how to swing a cutlass.

*Keep that blade up!*

I grit my teeth and pull the door open, leaping to the left as Vargaard commanded me.

Stekkan's voice cuts off with a high note I'm sure he doesn't want anyone to remember.

*"Bunch of fool talk anyway,"* Vargaard mutters in my mind and then he's moving, leaping forward to meet the creature roaring through the door.

The monster's a sailor – or he was a sailor. He's not even a man, now. He's cracked down the middle like a half-hatched egg, purple smoke billowing out the top of him and forming a giant-sized blob of violence and hate.

If I could shrink back, I would. If I could avoid this fight, I would. But if I shrink, all that's left is to be tossed overboard and hunted and killed by a pretty princess and her smoke unicorn. So, I grit my teeth, brace my feet, and say to the Duke, "Hold that light higher!"

My shadow streaks out long and harsh before me and Vargaard – my shadow bodyguard, and the ancient warrior who was trapped in a sword and now has chosen to be trapped in my shadow – rises, grabs the creature by its split skull, and wrenches it in a way that makes my throat seize and choke like it wants to spill yesterday's breakfast out. Thankfully, I had no breakfast yesterday. Instead, I lift the cutlass a touch higher, in front of my face.

*"Step now and slash,"* he says and he flings his victim so that all I have to do is strike an already falling body as he lays into the other three, dancing to strike one and then spin into a kick to the next, blow for blow, for blow.

The first man – if you can call him that – must have been the one they picked up at Saltfast – poor fools that they are. I grit my teeth, try not to cry, and hack the cutlass into his neck. I don't want to see what I've done so I don't look. Vargaard will tell me if I'm in trouble and the wet sound – like rain-soaked wood under an axe – feels far too real to me. So, too, does the spatter of something hot hitting my hands.

The gasp of the sailors behind me joins my hot panting as I fight an external battle with an already dead sailor and an internal battle with my own fear.

But I've seen worse. I've done worse.

*"Up and spin to the right,"* Vargaard warns and I'm fast to obey – I've learned that much, at least. He needs me to move when he says move and jump when he says jump. I'm not the real monster hunter – he is. I'm just the one who throws the shadow he lives within. *"You are everything – my sun, my stars, my light in a black universe."*

I might feel warm and fuzzy at that, but he says it between the loud crack of one once-sailor's neck and the cry of pain from the other. A fist flies at me from the third sailor and I barely duck under it, breath trapped in my throat.

Air whooshes over me and he's so close I can see when his chest constricts and my inky shadow morphs into a young warrior – corporeal in that single moment of violence, the only time he can be. His beautiful face ripples into fury and then he *rips* and I turn my face to the side hoping not to see what the inside of a man's shoulder looks like. His scream deafens me, ringing through my head like an accusation and then he slips, sliding across the blade of the cutlass I grip in both hands.

I don't like cutlasses, I don't like how mine slices right through his shirt and flays the skin from his white, stark ribs.

I'm going to throw up. I just know it.

*"Hold it in. Be strong. We'll get you a proper straight blade."*

Because yes, my inability to wield the cutlass is the part worrying me. Of course.

This sailor is past saving now, too, left to gurgle his way into death and now there are only two.

Wait.

One.

The snap I heard was Vargaard snapping a neck. Its owner lies in a twisted heap. His chest is still. Both he and the one who flayed himself on my blade are newly sick or possessed or whatever you might call catching the Scourge. They haven't shifted to the next stage yet – not like the corricle who was first to the door.

One more. My mouth is dry as I spin to face my enemy. My shadow already lunges and darts to bring him to grips. I raise the bloody sword and nearly jump back.

The sailor rips down the middle before my eyes, skull splitting apart neatly, eyes rolling back in his head. He makes a cry somewhere between a scream and a moan just before the rip breaches his throat and now my knees are trembling and I'm never going to be able to hold it together.

Screams ring out from behind me along with the sound of flight and oh, I wish I was fleeing, too.

*"Hold your courage. Steady now."*

I grit my jaw. I stay steady. If I flinch, Vargaard might miss his chance.

Smoke begins to bubble up from the corricle's shell, bright and yellow like a fir branch caught aflame, and then Vargaard slams his two halves back together like a maid beating a rug against itself.

Once. Twice. Three times.

The smoke scatters in puffs.

*"Sword up!"*

He pivots and jams the split creature onto my blade, severing its head and I am trembling now from foot to head as the sword is wrenched from my grip and clatters to the ship deck.

*"Yes. No more cutlasses, I think."*

Pain shudders up my arms from the violence of losing the sword. But I'm still on my feet and no one else is.

*"That makes you the winner."*

Or at least, it makes me still alive. And as long as Jendaya is alive, too, it binds me to the one thing I'm certain of – that I must stop her, even if it means killing a thousand of these creatures.

*"It surely will."*

"Even if it means chasing her across the country all the way to the capital."

*"That, also, is a certainty."*

Even if it means my belly never settles again.

*"Perhaps we'll find an herb for that."*

I'll do what I must. And so will my living shadow.

*"Always, Ilsaletta."*

From behind me, there's a wheezing cough and then the duke says brightly, "See? I told you she's a monster hunter. Do you have any more around here?"

# Chapter Two

"You need to stop calling me a monster hunter," I say as I struggle up to sitting. I'm in the captain's bed. He gave it to me to sleep at Stekkan's insistence and since I hadn't slept since the night before last, I took it and let myself fall under the crashing waves of somnolence, my shadow hovering over me bent on my protection.

"And what else would I call you?" Stekkan asks mildly. He's sitting in the chair opposite the bed – a squat creation with a tight cloth seat and legs in the form of the letter X, but with each leg fixed tightly to the deck. It's light and clever just like the captain himself. "You find monsters where no one would expect them to be, and you slay them. It takes a lot out of you – but who can fault you for that?"

Clearly, he cannot. He waits, though, and this time I know what he wants from me. And because he negotiated passage with the captain and arranged for the long sleep I just had, I give it to him.

"Thank you, Stekkan, Duke of Catterail," I say, and I really do mean it. "Thank you for saving my life, and getting me into the boat, for hailing this ship, and for negotiating sleep for me."

"You're welcome," he says, and he sounds pleased. He clears

his throat before I can say anything else and his pleased look fades to one that seems more nervous. "And now, before you go charging out onto the deck like I know you want to, there are things I want to discuss with you."

*"Of course there are,"* Vargaard complains from the sliver of shadow behind me. *"He has an endless number of things he wants to discuss."*

I may never broker a peace between them, but I would not ever jeopardize my friendship with my shadow – he has become like another skin to me – and I find Stekkan to be a friend in a world where I've lost all my other friends.

"This ship will take us to Seamark, the closest Cragspearean port," Stekkan says.

This much, I know. I was awake for his short, sharp negotiation. I nod, showing him I'm following his thoughts, as I run my fingers through my hair to release the tangles.

He pauses and something lights in his eyes that Vargaard doesn't like.

My shadow growls quietly like a dog sensing danger. It's not the first time I'm glad no one but me can hear him. I feel my cheeks growing hot at that thought and busy myself with smoothing my dress and coat. They're both blood-flecked. Do I dare try to wash them with nothing else to wear? I left the rags I'd escaped in on the beach when I donned this stolen dress.

I open the bag hopefully as Stekkan continues, sounding a little more awkward now.

"We don't dare let them leave Seamark," he says, his tone regretful.

"What?" I ask, looking up sharply. I've collected Princess

Jendaya's bag from the deck and I'm looking through it. I pull a washing cloth from the depths and wet it in the captain's pitcher beside the bed.

"They carry the sickness now, whether they know it or not. You said it can be up to two days to fully infect someone, correct? They picked up the first sailor from Saltfast only yesterday. He'd infected those other three by the time they reached our beach – fast enough that they had to drop sail and anchor to bring every hand into the work of dealing with them. That's faster than two days."

"It *can* take two days," I say, washing my face thoroughly with the cloth before turning to dab my dress and coat. "Or as little as an hour."

"Well, then," he says and he seems poleaxed.

"How long has it been since I fell asleep?"

His eyes snap back to me and his expression is sickly. "Four hours."

"And you haven't left the cabin since?" I press.

He curses and I feel the same way. With a sigh, I stop trying to clean my dress.

"We don't dare let them infect the rest of the world," he says, firmly.

"And you and me?" I ask, my eyebrows rising. "What about us?"

"If we're infectious even now, after we've survived, then there's no hope for anyone," he says grimly. "It's my thought that we should continue on as you wanted to – to Swordheart to warn the king."

"We can't possibly beat Jendaya to the capital now," I say and it's like I haven't even slept. My heart is racing, and my leg is kicking rhythmically like I can channel all my nerves into that one repeating movement and my eyes can't take in any detail before skittering to the next. They're noting the wood paneling, and the hooded candle, and the drapery over the round window in the stern of the ship as if I need to use these things to fight or flee.

Stekkan pulls at his slightly curling hair. "I don't know what else to do."

"She was clear that if we had all seven swords we could stop her," I say.

"What seven swords?" He pauses in his attempt to go bald before thirty.

"Mine and six others."

"The one you used to have that she stole, you mean?"

"Yes, that one." Our words are tight and pointed. We're looking deep into each other's eyes as if we hope we might see something there more than mirrored worry.

"And you don't know where the others are?"

I shake my head, but my mind is racing. Who would know? How could I find out?

"Then that's more a fool's gamble than racing the princess to Swordheart."

I bite my lip.

*"It's still the only plan we have,"* Vargaard puts in. He's so transparent in the bright cabin that I can hardly see him at all.

He seems thoughtful, all the same. And, of course, he would be. If anyone knows these swords and their lore, it's him. After all, he's lived in one for over a millennium – if my guess is right.

"Then we'd best get on deck and be sure the crew still lives," I say with a sigh. I'll think of something. Somehow. That's what I do best – think. And read. "Perhaps there will be answers in the library at Seamark."

"Before you go up, there's one more thing to talk about," the duke says and he's not looking at me, he's suddenly very interested in what's outside the window and he's chewing his lip like he can mash the words into submission.

After a long moment, I speak when I realize he's having trouble with it.

"If you're going to tell me you're sad about the priest, then you should know that I am, too," I say gently, standing up. Vargaard stands with me.

*"The priest collected a hefty debt from you before wasting it all by dying at Jendaya's hand. You owe him no more sorrow."*

And yet he would get more from me. I just couldn't seem to forget him. I wish she hadn't killed him. I wish he hadn't trusted her.

"What?" the duke looks at me then, surprise evident in his wide eyes. He's just as pretty as ever, his lashes so dark that it looks like someone lined those wide brown eyes with charcoal. "Oh, no, rest his poor soul. No, it was about a more practical matter."

He stands abruptly and I'm surprised by how real he feels when his warmth meets mine. I realize I haven't been this near a living human who wasn't trying to kill me since Stekkan stitched me up. My hand strays to the scar on my back unconsciously. I'm still shocked that it healed so quickly, though my newer wounds won't heal that fast. Not without the Mercy Sword. I miss it already.

"I'm a practical man, though you might not think so," Stekkan says, smiling crookedly as he flicks lint from his worn canary coat. "And so, I present to you a practical problem. We're surrounded by monsters, and I'm meant to marry their creator."

"Don't worry," I say, trying to be reassuring. "We'll find a way to stop them."

I put a hand on his arm. Is that too much? But he looks so nervous.

*"It's too much. Don't give him the wrong idea."*

To Vargaard, a smile or a crust of bread given freely would be the wrong idea.

*"He slows you down. You should leave him at Seamark."*

"Of course," Stekkan says but his cheeks only stain brighter. "But what I mean to say is that you should reconsider marrying me."

"What?" I freeze. To my surprise, Vargaard says nothing. I expected disdain.

"It's convenient for us both," Stekkan hurries to point out and his tongue seems thick in his mouth because his words stumble. "For me, you are a minor noble and my family can't deny you. If I marry you before I see them, it will nullify my betrothal to Jendaya. And in a land of monsters, marrying a monster hunter is a clever choice."

"I'm not a monster hunter," I say, stunned that he's offering this again when his neck is no longer on the line – sort of.

"So, you say," he says, trying a shy smile. It's not working. "But this is also clever for you. You've left your home and fortune in ruins. Your father, Divine Sovereign willing, may someday return, but he may also be taken by the sea as those in his place sometimes are. You're destitute. But with me, you would have comfort, and wealth, and a home."

I open my mouth to remind him that I won't marry him, but he holds up a single brown hand and smiles at me a little wider.

"I know you're going to reject me, but don't just yet. Think on it. You're a practical girl and it's such a very practical solution that I know you'll come to see it the same way. You just need time to think without anyone dying in front of you while you're sorting out your priorities."

I give him my longest, driest look. This would be the point where I'd expect Vargaard to say something. Vargaard, who almost kissed me last night. Vargaard, who other than being very helpful in that monster fight this morning has been fairly quiet ever since.

Vargaard? I ask in my mind but receive nothing back.

That's …unexpected. But it's unfair for me to assume he should be at my beck and call like a hunting dog. He's a man, not a tool. No matter how he regards himself.

I take a long breath to calm myself and say to Stekkan. "Let's go see what we find on deck, shall we?"

One battle at a time. It's all I can manage. I can't worry about more than that.

# NAKURAKI

She can't marry. And especially not a duke who stands by and lets her fight his battles for him. If she should marry it should be a marriage to a god among men. A man with prowess in battle so he can muster armies at her request and lead them as she directs. He should be a scholar who can advise her – but one not so foolish as to think he knows better than her. He should be a monk, sworn to asceticism, who drinks no strong drink lest he fail her, and has never indulged himself in the pleasures of the flesh.

A memory flashes across my mind – fast and sweet. Bright joy in my friend's eyes, the smell of jasmine in the air as he peered through the green leaves watching for his bride.

"She arrives, Vargaard," he says in a hush.

I feel a throb of happiness all over again, remembering Caspan Hedrend Ak'Genar, who I helped to hold off hordes of barbarians from rolling over the hills he called his kingdom.

I shake myself at that. Even such a man as that would not be worthy.

And such a man does not exist.

But though I feel her questing for my mind, I do not answer

her thoughts. If I speak now, it will only be in the howl of despair. The frustrated fury of a spirit who shall never hold a body again.

I let the fury flail me from within, let the ache of disappointment stain me yet another shade of purple despair, and I wait to do what I do best – guard my Vali. See her safe. Lift her to glory.

# Chapter Three

Stepping out of the ship's cabin turns out to be more difficult than I expected. I push my weight against the door but it catches, wedged on something beyond it.

"The door should open inward," Stekkan says from beside me, weathered seaman that he is. "It's not safe in a storm if it opens outward. What if water filled the passageway and trapped the captain inside?"

I don't have time to critique the ship's builder and I don't have the bulk to open the door easily. I might ask for help, but Vargaard is still playing his silent game. Instead, I arch an eyebrow at Stekkan and we both put our shoulders to the door and throw our weight against it.

It opens slowly, binding and creaking before finally opening enough for us to squeeze out. Thank the seas, Stekkan is not a large man. He'll ease through this as easily as I do.

I'm careful to snatch up the cutlass before we exit, holding it up as Vargaard taught me. It's that preparation that keeps my heart from seizing at what has held the door.

Sprawled across the deck – dead as yesterday's catch – is the captain. I clench my jaw hard at the sight and swallow down gorge at the smell of him. It's his captain's coat that has bound under the door. Was he on his way here to tell us something?

My heart beats double-time at the thought.

"Wha – ?" Stekkan starts to say but I throw up a hand to silence him.

The silence of the ship seems less friendly than it did a moment ago. Above us, something creaks in the wind and, in my mind's eye, I'm seeing an entire ship of the dead – or worse.

It's the worse that worries me.

And just like that, Vargaard is back. His voice is deep and thick like expensive velvet.

*"Walk on the balls of your feet so you don't make a sound. Take your time. Clumsiness will alert your enemies."*

Was he certain there would be enemies?

*"In a crew like this? Knowing that ten in a hundred men are truly evil – in an average population – how many would you think are evil on a ship with a crew of twenty?"*

Two?

His snort in my mind is disbelieving.

I slip along the passageway, concentrating on the creak of the ship, the shudder as something moves along ropes above. The scent – mostly brine, but something is burning.

The duke sounds like a half-grown pup behind me, banging into everything along the way like he has the kind of tail they might dock for him. I turn long enough to give him a pointed look and he colors, holding his hands up in a gesture of peace.

He leans against the side of the passage, watching the captain's corpse as if he expects that grey skin to flush to life again.

I try not to look at it. Even if I wasn't occupied with sneaking through this ghost ship, I wouldn't want to see what death has done to the man. I barely remember him as more than a whisper behind my back, and I don't want to replace that whisper with this hollowed shell.

The ladder is before me now. Up or down. Below is the scent of something burning. Above will be the tiller and whoever may still sail this ship.

*"Above. Control the situation first. Limit damage second."*

That seemed reasonable. I could ask Vargaard later why he hid when I was being proposed to but emerged when the fighting started.

*"My advice on amorous situations is not as sound as my advice in combat."*

And that was all? He had nothing else to say on the matter?

*"Your left side is your blind side. You pull to the right without meaning to. You should be mindful of the left so an enemy cannot take advantage of the weakness."*

Not exactly the opinion I was looking for.

*"And yet it is exactly what you need. If we could break you of that, you would be more formidable in every encounter with hostile forces."*

The ladder squeaks under my weight and I pause, but when no other sound follows, I must continue. I hate how that means my head will be at foot level when I come through the hatch to the main deck. Someone could kick me. Or chop my head right off.

*"It's good to know these things, but don't imagine them if you can help it. Imagine stepping up strong and immovable. Sometimes our thoughts taint the world around us, and I'd not have you taint yours with poor fortune."*

I do as he says, thinking of success as I launch myself – fast and strong – up the final steps of the ladder and to the deck.

I'm greeted by the dead. And I don't understand how there can be so many of them up here when I was sleeping below and heard not a thing. And what of Stekkan? Did he not say he sat by me as I slept? Did he hear nothing? Or did he hear and do nothing?

The chill in my bones has nothing to do with the wind blowing over the decks.

I pick my way slowly, careful to avoid the heaped bodies. I'm counting. And it is counting that shows me they didn't all just fall over dead. Most have no signs of violence on them, they simply lie slumped over, glazed eyes staring up at the cloud-dappled sky and the top of the mast. Lips parted in surprise. Like Betsy and the cook and the others in my house, they've been killed before they realized they were sick. And all because they picked up a traveler in Saltfast. Another sailor just like them.

I swallow against a dry throat. This is why Princess Jendaya came to Saltfast. An experiment in an out-of-the-way place. And here are some of her results. She wanted to know how fast it would spread to other cities and countries. This is how fast. As fast as a sleek merchant ship that pauses to pick up a fellow in sailcloth trousers.

*"This is a problem. Any survivors will need to be dispatched."*

And then what? Even my mental voice is trembling. I don't

know these people. They don't hurt me to look at like the people in my town did. But they ingrain themselves in my mind for a different reason – fail in what I'm trying to accomplish, and this will be the entire world.

I can't see the tiller from here – or at least I can, but there are two dead bodies slumped over the rail in front of it, so I can't see if there's a man behind it.

*"Their throats were slashed. Inexpertly. I'd say that whatever husk killed them isn't fully taken over by the other side yet."*

Above me, the sail snaps and my spine straightens with it. I look up, up, up.

Nothing but sail and clouds and the scream of a bird.

That scream echoes something that's screaming inside me.

The timbers in the boat creak, and it leans slightly to the side. Maybe that means there's no one at the tiller. Maybe it means everyone is dead. Maybe they were all neither good nor evil.

*"You have to find out."*

I could just stand here for a moment.

*"And if they have a crossbow? A blow dart?"*

I swallow. I don't want to die here among the stinking dead.

I start my creep across the deck again.

*"Move with the roll of the ship, let the creaking disguise your movement."*

Did whoever was at the tiller see me? My eyes strain to try to see through the bodies, but I can't see more than shadows. I look over each shoulder, scanning the deck, but then I have to do it again. My eyes are just skimming over things. My brain doesn't seem able to analyze what I see.

*"That's your fear. You must master it. We're almost to the ladder to the aft deck. Hold your courage tightly."*

I take a deep breath, trying to obey and grasp the rail beside the ladder. Vargaard is trapped behind me. He shouldn't be. We should be sailing directly away from the sun. When did the ship change course?

*"You won't be able to sneak from here. Climb all in one big burst. If he has a bow or crossbow, hit the deck immediately."*

I gather in one more breath.

"Tell the captain. Tell the captain!" someone calls, and I jump, my whole body shivering. Who was that? They sounded high pitched enough that they might be being tortured – but we'd heard no cries or screams. "Pox! Pox!"

*"Go now!"*

Heart in my throat, I leap up the ladder and scan the aft deck.

Like the main deck, it's heaped with bodies – these ones despatched in violence. There's blood splashed everywhere and viscera I never wanted to contemplate in gobs nearby. I feel light-headed. There's something black swimming across my vision.

*"Ilsaletta. Vali. Light of my heart. Hold yourself steady."*

I gulp down air and see the two living left among the dead. To my relief, neither has a crossbow or any other missile shooter. It's just the first mate leaning wearily over the tiller and on his shoulder is a blue and gold macaw. I've never seen one before except in drawings in my father's book *"The Fauna of Poco Pera."*

The Macaw scratches its head with one foot as if it sees piles of bodies every day.

"Hello," it says.

The first mate looks up, green-faced, to give me a sickly smile.

"I didn't kill the parrot," he says like he should get a prize for that. "I had to kill the others. They were for pressing on to Seamark and we can't have that. Even I know that. I have family in Seamark."

He leaned to the side and vomited loudly – which should have made me feel ill, but the blood coating him to the elbows and decorating the tiller was so much worse than a lost breakfast.

The parrot screamed, "Mercy! Mercy! Mercy!"

More than anything else that made me want to run.

"*My shadow doesn't reach from here,*" Vargaard said grimly. Sure enough, his shadow reached out behind me in the hot late, afternoon sun.

"Where do you sail, then?" I asked mildly. I didn't want to go closer. I was getting little lights dancing across my vision just thinking about it. Maybe if I could make him turn the ship, Vargaard would find a better position from which to strike.

"*Good thinking.*"

"Anywhere but Seamark." His eyes shoot up to me. "You don't plan to stop me, too, do you?"

"Did these others try to stop you?" I ask mildly. I don't think he'll turn the ship. Maybe I can gain his confidence.

"They started dropping – where they stood. No sound. No cry. Just falling like they'd gone to sleep standing up. All but Matty and Dulpepper."

"Those two on the railing?" I suggest.

"Ha! No! Those are Marco and Patrice. I cut their throats as my banner. A flag to sail under. Anyone with a spyglass sees those cods and they'll hop away right fast. They were mostly dead already. I can add you to the flag if you want. Better way to go than when we run out of water."

"We're going to run out of water?" I ask – still trying to be careful in how I talk. I take a step forward and immediately regret it. Something slides under my foot. These remains covering the aft deck must be Matty and Dulpepper.

"Don't take that calm tone with me," the mate says, eyes going wild. "Don't take it. Matty took it and look at him now! Him and Dulpepper both trying to talk me around. Trying to tell me to keep sailing east. Even my own mind rising against me. I feel it. It's bubbling up. I'll lash myself to the mast. I'll not let it take my family, too. Just me and Mercy here to die of thirst together. But first, cut your throat. I forgot that one."

And then he leaps, clearing the tiller so fast I barely get my blade up as the macaw screeches, "Mercy! Mercy! Mercy!" and launches herself over me.

Vargaard materializes so close in front of me I can almost feel the muscles of his shoulders bunching in front of my face as he blocks my attacker, sending him stumbling. My Nakuraki's shadow sword bursts out, splitting the flesh of the sailor and I'd never know now if he was good and pushed to do bad things or evil and still just human enough not to want to kill his own family.

*"He's evil. Down to the core."*

My Nakuraki doesn't need my blade for the final blow, but that doesn't mean I'm not panting and breathless by the time Vargaard is done with him.

*"Easy now. Easy, my girl. The threat is passed – up here at least. We'll launch the ship's boat and flee. I'll let none harm you now or ever."*

But I can tell that he is injured by how he holds his arm close to his chest. Will he heal without the sword to sleep in?

*"I can sleep in your shadow, and I will – but not until we're off this rig."*

I straighten to look around me and agree. I can't sail this ship on my own, and even if I could, I don't have the stomach for it. I stumble my way to the ship's boat, my hands splaying over its rough-hewn side in relief. Still here. With oars, too.

I should raid the captain's cabin and the galley first. I have no idea where we are or how far away Seamark is. We'd need maps and instruments. And water. We'd need that.

Something touches my shoulder and I yelp, scooting away. It's only a wide-eyed Stekkan there. His hands are full of maps and instruments. He has my bag from Jendaya, a pair of full water skins, and another leather satchel over one shoulder, and the fierce macaw on the other.

"Don't kill me," he stammers.

"Oh good," I say, sagging slightly. "You brought the maps."

# Chapter Four

"You're going to have to get rid of the bird," I say as we sail toward the city. The wind snaps around me, salty and exhilarating forcing alertness so that I notice every bright flash of green and wash of bubbling foam as our boat dips and reels its way through the drink's embrace.

I wonder if this is what has lured my father out again and again, away from his young wife and tiny daughter, away from his comfortable home on the rock, this siren song of death and freedom that so many of my people have followed over the generations that we took on the very name of the thing – Redtide.

Stekkan and I had rigged a small sail and mast in the ship's boat, not trusting our own backs to row what should have been a two-day journey by ship. We'd been clever to do that, but even so, after a full day and a night in the boat, I'd panicked twice about whether we were reading the map right and whether the captain had charted the course correctly before we finally sighted Seamark in the looking glass. I'm still folding and refolding the maps. They're beautifully drawn on thick paper – expensive, beautiful, and worthy of respect. But even perfect maps are only as good for navigation as the people reading them.

It's Vargaard's resonant voice whispering comfort hour after hour that's calmed me through the worst of the doubt.

*"You're good at this,"* he told me when I was certain we were lost. *"You will figure it out but only if you calm down. Worry dulls the senses. Anxiety saps the strength."*

And then, when I thought I was on the right course, but couldn't be sure.

*"I was on a ship once that lost its way, and we found a flat island with nothing but squat birds and their leavings."*

"Is that meant to be encouraging?"

*"We stopped, hoping to take on freshwater, though there was none, and at the center of the flat rocks was a tiny plaque so old we had to scrape the seaweed from its face. It said, "Here lies Trychen, said to be a god but cut into these five pieces."*

I had shivered. How terrible, to find a grave when you thought you were dying.

And he had laughed in my mind. *"'Twas worse for those aboard who had been praying to him the last seven-day. For the people of that place worshipped Trychen and threw fish back in the water in his name."*

They thought he truly was a god, I realized. What beliefs did I have that would crumble like that?

Do you worship something, Vargaard? I'd asked in my mind. Perhaps I would pray to his god.

He'd been quiet a long time.

*"Sometimes I wonder if we can help what we worship, or if we are bent by the hands of what created us in such a way that we can only worship what founded us. A line can, possibly, be drawn from*

*the acts of the hands to the heart of the man and from there to the
one who formed him first."*

And who formed you? I wanted to say, but I stayed silent
because the secret of the book I'd read before Jendaya stole it
back was seared into my soul – that only a truly innocent man
could be trapped and made a Nakuraki. That he was punished
for an evil heart he'd never even had. Did he worship something
– perhaps in error – that had bent him into both shame and
service?

And he was silent, too, haunted, perhaps, as I was, by truths
too hard to name.

But now, with the city in sight and the fragrant wind in our
favor, we're getting close to shore and I'm beginning to think of
practicalities.

"The bird," I say again, raising my brows.

I give Stekkan a long hard look. He's lounging at the front
of the boat, the spray keeping his stubbled jaw and short hair
perpetually highlighted with sea spray. Combined with the bird,
it makes him look like a pirate who's barely slipped the noose
– devilish in the most attractive way. The kind of trouble any
woman would welcome in her life. He picks idly at a tear in his
ruined doublet. It clings to the lithe muscle of his form like a
kid glove clings to the hand, leaving absolutely nothing under its
semblance of decency to the imagination.

I sniff. There's nothing we can do about the canary jacket or
the clinging clothing, but we can at least dispense with the bird
and *try* to go unnoticed.

"And how would you suggest I do that?" he asks as the macaw
screams back at a lunging seagull. They've been engaged in that
exact argument since noon. Macaw against seagull in a fight to

the death. "She won't want to leave the boat. We're the only solid thing she can sit on."

*"He could drown it or break its neck. It will be a terrible hindrance in battle. I have seen war-trained shrikes which dive down and pluck out a man's eyes, but this showy thing is just like the man who holds it – useless."*

Vargaard's opinion is definite, but I refuse to voice his suggestion. I don't actually want to kill the creature. Or at least, I don't right now. Give me a few more hours of this and I might.

"Mercy! Mercy!" screams the bird in that terrible half-growl half-scream, as if she can read our thoughts.

"Besides," Stekkan says, reaching up to ruffle the macaw's feathers. "This bird could live longer than me."

*"It certainly will if he carries it with him. It will draw the attention of everyone within a hundred leagues."*

"We can't afford to maintain a bird," I say coolly.

"We can't afford not to," Stekkan replies, leaning back to stretch a little more. He's surprisingly well-muscled for someone who spends every free moment sitting idly, and I find myself noticing his strength. He preens slightly under my gaze, not realizing that I'm not admiring him so much as that I'm envious of the masculine form that gives him such natural power – power I could use in wielding the sword. I'm ill-suited to the task I've been thrust into. Though, perhaps, all that has ended now.

*"It has not. There will be more battles to fight. There always are after you pick up a sword. You may leave it, but it never leaves you."*

"You're the monster hunter," Stekkan says with a warm smile and heavy-lidded eyes. He's definitely mistaking my regard. "I'm the duke – but don't tell anyone. Tell them I'm a minstrel." At my nod, he continues. "When we come upon monsters or anything that needs killing, I'll leave that to you."

"How generous. And map reading?" I suggest. I'm the one who has been navigating for us. And I've been sailing the boat because I read a book on how to sail which apparently makes me the most experienced of the three of us. The first time Stekkan tried, he nearly capsized us.

"Certainly – anything seafaring," the duke concedes with a lady-winning smile. "But when it comes to social matters, you'd best leave that to me."

"Social matters?" I say, half-smiling, raising an eyebrow. Sometimes I can't believe his audacity. I look away to watch the shore growing larger. The relief I feel at the sight of land makes my eyes tear up a little. Who would have thought I'd love solid ground under my feet with such passion? Everything seems greener and bluer as I watch it approach.

"The bird will distract from our ragged clothing. Macaws are still a novelty – even in seaports. And we need people to remember her, not the girl in a bloodstained ballgown, or the man in the tattered duke's doublet."

I frown, but he makes sense.

*"Even I have to concede that makes sense. The best way to hide is in plain sight."*

"Agreed," I say, eventually.

"And if you leave that to me, then also leave to me the matter of procuring fresh clothing, mounts, supplies, and rooms at an inn."

There's no way he can manage all that. But there's no way I can, either, so I say, "Also agreed."

Which is how I find myself four hours later, with crowds of people pressed so tightly around us that I fear I might panic and draw the ridiculous cutlass from the scabbard I stole as we fled.

"This fair bird's a real beauty and worth her salt, I can tell you! She can speak in four languages," Stekkan is saying loudly to the people whose bodies – and frankly, smell – are pressing me into him. I cough out the scent of rotting fish and flesh, only to drag it back in with the next breath. Stekkan puts an arm companionably over my shoulder and I tense. My eyes feel wider than the crowd. This is not how I expected our landing here to go. Maybe Vargaard was right. Maybe we should have killed the bird. I don't like any of this. What if we're contagious? What if we infect them, too?

*"Try to twist to look behind you. You need to scan the crowd."*

Vargaard sounds as tense as I feel. My shadow is ragged and barely there, mixed in the shadows of so many others.

Scan for what?

*"Anything out of the ordinary?"*

My chest feels tight. How will I know what's out of the ordinary in a place I've never been?

*"Start by looking for anyone ill."*

To my relief, Seamark is untouched by the scourge. I'm not as relieved by the crowds we draw as we move our way from the brightly colored busy docks to the even busier and more colorful merchant shops that follow up the cliff-side city. The streets are a maze of switchbacks set into the white chalk cliffs, one brightly painted shopfront merging into the next with nothing but a new color – raspberry now instead of robin's egg or lime instead of eggplant – to distinguish one from the next.

*"See that man sliding in behind the woman wearing red?"*

He looks normal.

*"Exactly. He's a thief. He's practiced in staying out of notice. Can you spot another like him?"*

I shift in place, looking.

This city is so full of running feet and shouting voices, of people selling bright wares and tossing gleaming coins, of snatches of song and whistled jolly-making, of shining catches of briny fish hauled up onto the docks, and wide-bellied merchants tapping stubbled chins as they judge the haul. Life bubbles out of every door of this place like a plant growing out of a too-small pot.

And in the middle of it, I see a woman in plain clothes, hair pulled back, face so average I can barely remember the details after a first glance. She seems bored, and yet her eyes flicker from face to face. She's like the thief.

*"Good. Yes. We'll teach you awareness yet. Start by learning the crowd like that. Find the thieves. Find anyone pretending to be something they aren't."*

I like his task. It's better than letting my nerves eat away at me. I want to be moving. I want to be doing something other than just walking with Stekkan. This place hardly feels real after that ship of ghosts.

We've almost arrived at the tailor Stekkan is aiming for – fighting through all this joyful teeming vigor –  but every jostle of the crowd makes Vargaard more nervous. He's been unwilling to rest and restore himself and his injury only seems to make him more on edge.

"But until I am able to replace my guild jacket and lute, I fear

I cannot do her justice," Stekkan says grandly to the crowd as if they do not smell of sweat and garlic. As if *we* do not smell of bile and blood. "Come, find me tonight at the … *The Shield and* … what's the name of the inn I'm staying at?"

"The Shield and Crown?" someone calls out.

"That's the one!" he calls and sweeps me into the tailor's shop, whispering in my ear, "It's always the shield and something."

I don't bother shaking my head. It's always something, alright.

Stekkan has a private talk with the tailor while I bounce nervously from foot to foot. I need to get to the library as soon as possible. It will take days to find what I'm looking for there – and that's if I'm lucky. The sooner I start my research, the sooner it will see fruit.

*"We don't have to, you know. This is your chance to run. To leave for a safe place and avoid the scourge and the consequences of it. I know you've rejected the idea before, but you hold my soul in your shadow. I'd bear the guilt all my days if I did not offer you the chance to save yourself."*

I've already made this decision. I'm no warrior without Vargaard, but I can't stand aside and watch the world crumble like Saltfast did. I snatch a premade linen dress from a rack and bring it to where Stekkan and the tailor have their heads together.

"Can you afford this one?" I ask Stekkan without preamble. It's a dress suitable to a common shop girl. Well-made and clean, but unadorned. Probably the best he can afford – if he truly has funds as he claims. Likely he pilfered something from the ship without my noticing. But maybe – if I'm very lucky – the dress will prove clean enough to get me into a library.

The duke's macaw squawks and its gold-and-blue horror is

reflected in the faces of Stekkan and the tailor.

"Oh no, my lady, nothing but custom-made for you. I have a piece I can work over by tomorrow," the tailor says. I wonder what Stekkan has told him, but I don't want to waste time finding out.

*"Whatever it is, it's likely a lie. The man lies as easily as he smiles."*

"I can't wait until tomorrow. I need something now," I say, chin held up determinedly. And I need something we can afford. We can't afford custom work.

Stekkan snatches the dress from my hands. "They don't let commoners in the Royal Seamark Library, wife, and that's how you'd look in that common dress."

*"Wife?"* Vargaard's outrage is almost a roar. *"He'd claim such familiarity without your consent?"*

I want to roll my eyes at them both.

"I'll wear whatever you want, as long as I can leave for the library within the hour," I say, reasonably.

"I have just the thing," the tailor says brightly, lifting his creation.

"Mercy!" the macaw shrieks and for once I agree with her.

# NAKURAKI

Something has changed. I feel it in the back of my head. Something I can't quite discern.

I prod at the feeling, wary. It lies dead and unreachable like a lost limb in the back of my soul.

And in its place blooms something new – something that terrifies me.

I'm the first of my kind to attach myself to a mortal's shadow. I should not be surprised that it is changing me.

I reach for a scrap of memory. Something about a man full of happiness. I smell jasmine and see green leaves waving in the wind and then it's gone – ripped away from my grasp as if it never was.

It had been important. I can feel the shape of that, even if the memory has eluded me.

It takes the entire voyage – truncated as it is – to realize what has happened. Those other men I was are dead. And while their memories still trickle back to me, what they once were is beginning to rot in the back of my mind – a hundred other lives all slowly disintegrating as I am not just new for now, but new forever.

I smell the waft of their passing, feel them twitch within me as their memories rise and fade before they can be experienced. A wealth of lifetimes bubbling up like a corpse rotting beneath a pond.

What have I done?

# CHAPTER FIVE

*"Next time, don't tell him he can dress you in anything,"* Vargaard says.

I almost think he is sulking. He's been pacing in front of me like a cat locked in the house on a full moon. It's hard to concentrate on what I'm reading when he's like that.

Three steps along my shadow – made long by the tall, peaked windows in sets of three along the library wall – and then three steps back. His clothing and hairstyles flick, flick, flicker with his agitation. He moves from barbarian to prince to pirate. His lovely face is lined too deeply for the simple offense of a dress.

It is an outrageous dress. Stekkan seems incapable of choosing anything else. A raspberry silk outer wrapper sheathes yet another faux breastplate that wouldn't protect anything – why even make these things? Fortunately for me, there are trousers over my legs. Apparently, it's the latest fashion to look like an ill-equipped warrior.

I miss my simple flowing dresses from home but not enough to complain. I have work to do. And it's not a complete loss. I kept my father's coat in Jendaya's stolen bag with the maps and navigation instruments.

Besides, I needed to get into this library. I was just lucky Stekkan was able to afford something. He's out again now, gathering other supplies and horses and more clothing. And a lute for his minstrel disguise, which I'm sure I'll be sorry to hear him play.

I shake my head, but I have no time for distractions. I'm deep into this book – the fifth volume of *"Famous Weapons of the Coastal Cities."* And there's nothing. No hints on where these other swords might be – the ones Jendaya said were necessary to defeat her glowing green gem from spitting the scourge everywhere. No references to the gem, either. No mentions or comments about anyone using the swords or keeping them somewhere. Whoever hid them, hid them well.

*"Or perhaps they are lost. That was always a possibility,"* Vargaard says, pausing in his pacing. *"What will you do if they're lost?"*

I'll find them. I must. I'd never thought I'd be like a person in a story on a long quest to find a lost talisman. But perhaps that will be me.

I have no idea how to be a treasure hunter.

*"It's simple enough. First, discover where the treasure is. Second, go to that place. Third, take it. Fourth, kill any who try to stop you."*

The way he said it made it sound like thieving.

*"It is thieving. But with a pretty name."*

I didn't want to be a thief.

*"I didn't want to be a murderer."*

I look up at him for the first time since the beach, since he tried to kiss me – or did kiss me – or whatever you called what we did when we can't even touch each other. I blink and he's right in front of me like he's been there all along and I'm swallowing down a lump in my throat and how did this breastplate thing get so tight?

*"Neither of us wanted this."*

Does he mean the violence, or does he mean our – friendship? Romance? Whatever this thing is that twists my guts into knots.

He's so close that he could kiss me again. I can't help myself. I lick my lips. Even knowing he'll never taste them, that it doesn't matter that they're dry, that this can go nowhere. But is that true? I've read so many tales where the impossible happened. So many stories where the frog came to life at the princess's kiss, or the beast became a prince when beauty fell in love with him.

I'm no beauty.

I'm certainly no princess.

And yet I can't help myself. Hope flares in me like the first lighting of a torch. If he could leave the sword to enter my shadow – could he leave the shadow to enter my world?

*"Don't."*

Don't what?

His shadow eyes are deep wells of sadness.

*"Don't wish for what cannot be. I am not here to leave you empty. I'm here to guard your hidden treasures."*

So, he's not going to kiss me again. It must have been relief that broke him down the first time. He'll not bend again.

I smile slightly, hiding the disappointment for his sake and to salve my pride and unsure of what reply to make. It's easier to hide my glowing cheeks in my book.

And that's when I finally see it – right here under my finger on the crumbling-edged yellow page.

*"It is rumored that the Seven Swords found their way to the coast, though such claims have remained unproven. Each guardian is sworn to secrecy on pain of death – and knowing that, who would agree to house a monster with no praise or reward to tempt him into it? There are some who claim these noble souls save them for a time of tumult and cataclysm. I find those claims hard to swallow and yet Ghrenharedin gave them credence and wrote about them in his* "Memoirs of the Chalk Coasts."

I slam the tome closed, choking on the dust it kicks up, and I'm back to the shelves at a run. I have the library to myself. The somnolent keeper leans over a ledger at the front desk, catching up on a thousand years of naps in a single day. When we entered this morning, he was so confused his only comment to me was, "Back already?" as if he knew me and I'd been there earlier that day. So long in a world of words has stolen his mind.

He does not wake when I lope by – just one more shuffling vermin scampering through his domain. I'm not concerned. There are answers here. I know it. I will find them.

I have *"Memoirs of the Chalk Coast"* on the reading table in minutes and I'm flipping pages as fast as I can, looking, looking, looking.

Books have always been a home to me. I'm on my home turf now and running faster through the books than my feet could ever take me.

I find something here.

*"The Memory Swords or the Seven Swords or the Swords of the Nakuraki – called by different names at different times – were meant to represent the arms of the goddess Ta'ana. Tenacity, tranquility,*

*mercy, wisdom, courage, spirituality, and generosity. Together, they formed too great a power, and so they were separated and scattered, meant to be sent to the seven corners of the earth. But such are the plans of man that they rarely come to fruition, and in the chaos of war and famine, they found their way to the same continent and some even to the same lands. It is said that the leaders of the nations gathered together to discuss what ought to be done with them when the long suffering of the Eighty Years War was complete. But no one potentate had the power to disburse them again, and none could agree to give up those they possessed. Where they have washed ashore since then, is a mystery for scholars better than I, for the secret is kept hidden from one keeper of the sword to the next, and despite all my seeking, I only found one."*

He found one? But *where* did he find it? And why did he not record it? I sank deeper into his records, searching, searching.

When I emerge, Stekkan is lounging on a leather chair beside my table, plucking idly at a lute with the bored expression of one who has been at it for hours.

"Back with us?" he asks, yawning. Even yawning, he looks too good to be around me. He's wearing a new canary jacket – this one even more ridiculous than the last. Someone has sewn it with embroidered feathers in brilliant blue that match the macaw on his shoulder. The macaw – ever the practical one – is asleep. "We both need a bed in the inn and a hot meal. It's halfway through the night, Lady Redtide."

"Go on without me," I say distractedly, though I have the grace to notice his gift. "And thank you for the light."

The lit lantern beside me wasn't there when I'd opened *"Memoirs"* and neither had the candelabra been.

"I lit those hours ago," he says, rolling his eyes. "Have you found any of the swords yet?"

"Not yet," I say. "But I think I'm getting close."

"You think you are," he says, strumming a new chord. He's actually very good, I realize. Perhaps he really can pose as a minstrel. "At least eat something. I have packs filled with provisions. There's even a very good cheese. I didn't expect to find *that* in this Cragspear backwater."

Stekkan gestures at a stack of packs beside him. When did he have time to find all that?

*"You've been here for many hours. Your focus is admirable."*

Stekkan's chords merge into a song I know. I've never heard it played so well.

*"He has to be good at something to balance out all the things he's bad at,"* Vargaard hasn't relaxed at all. He's still pacing. In fact, he seems more tense than ever. *"But he's right. You should eat something."*

"After I find this one thing," I say, my mind already racing ahead. "Then I'll eat. You should rest."

*"Wake me when you're done."* Vargaard agrees, and then vanishes.

I'm too busy to remember to ask how to wake him.

The next time I emerge, it's dawn.

Stekkan sleeps with his mouth open, snoring in the most lovely way. The macaw is awake but imitating him, so he sounds as if he sleeps, too.

No sign of Vargaard. Which is fine. He needs his rest. It's not his fault that I feel hollow when he's not around.

I'm back to hurrying through the stacks, scanning spines as fast as I can, the titles washing through my mind like a river. One sword is in Ghregorin. I've learned that much. And the last tome I read – a sixteen-thousand-page volume on the Eighty Years War – claimed a list had been made of the swords locations. Now, to find it. It should be in the "Chronicles of the Ledgermakers: Volume VII, Second Edition."

I'm shuffling through books when I realize how quiet it is. The walls of the library must be very thick. I can't even hear the sounds of the city. Could I hear them before? I can't remember.

Here it is! I find it, at last, as I'm coughing on dust. The library master should be ashamed of himself for letting the books get this dusty. Especially on a shelf so close to his desk. He's still slumped across it, so still, he looks like he's dead.

I shake my head and pick up my pace. If this book has the list, it's the end of our time here and Stekkan can go sleep in a proper inn.

I set the book on the library table – still careful, even in my haste. If you don't respect books, then they won't respect you, and it will *all* end poorly. Like that poor man they say was eaten by a book and had to live his days between the dictionary entries for *mammet* and *moron*.

And here it is!

*"Thus is the listings of those who came forward to confirm their possession of the swords in question, that is the swords of seven, the disputed items of the Eighty Years War. And thusly were they accounted for among the houses of the nobles, those houses being, firstly:*

*The Mercy Sword as claimed by Admiral Redtide of Craigspear."*

I felt a thrill at seeing my father's name and sword in the book – though it could as easily be my grandfather's name. He'd also been an Admiral.

*"The Tenacity Sword and claimed by Duke …*

The page was torn.

Frantic, I lifted it, shaking it. No piece fell out. Where were the other names?

I ran back to the shelf, combing through the dust but it was untouched other than that single book. And now I couldn't breathe because why hadn't I looked to see if the book had been disturbed? Why hadn't I at least tried to pay attention like Vargaard was teaching me?

Someone had stolen that page from the book. Someone either now or a long time ago. Someone who knew how important these swords were.

I couldn't breathe. I couldn't catch a breath.

I stumbled back to my reading table and closed the book, but I couldn't close my sense of defeat and the spiky certainty filling my veins that somehow this was my fault, too. I should have known this hours ago. I was too slow. Too occupied.

I needed fresh air. I couldn't breathe in this tight, closed library with the shelves that tottered six men high. I moved to blow out the candles and lantern but they'd burned out hours ago. It must be mid-morning by now.

My hands trembled from exhaustion and nerves as I drew in a steadying breath. I was just tired. Just hungry. Just thirsty. I needed to calm down.

I made my way – intentionally walking slowly – to the main

doors and threw them open. Fresh air filled my lungs and the sun warmed my face. I closed my eyes and let it fill me.

Something was not right.

The world remained silent.

I opened my eyes at the same moment that the macaw sailed over my head screaming, "Mercy! Mercy!"

She was the only one to so much as squawk. The silence around us was the silence of the dead.

# CHAPTER SIX

I reel where I stand, nearly losing my balance. It's too close to last time. Too close to the bodies piled in heaps in my courtyard.

The library steps spill down to the city square. I hadn't bothered noting the soaring stone architecture of the courthouse or the castle at the center of the city on my way here. My mind had been full of the task at hand. I only notice them now because I want to look at anything other than the hundreds of corpses scattered across the ground, slumped against walls and the low wall of the pool in the center of the square.

A scream catches in my throat and I clamp down hard on it, holding it in. Panic is trying to claw up my throat. Bad enough to find yourself at the center of a house filled with the dead. Worse to find yourself in the center of a city.

Wings flap as birds kick up from the masses of dead, unaffected. My hair batters my face, windblown, distracting. I blink dry eyes and try to still my skittering thoughts.

Deep breaths, Ilsaletta, I tell myself. Deep breaths.

But the breath I pull in already smells of death. I throw a hand over my nose and mouth and scan the dead. All their vibrant colors are faded. All their loud chatter snatched like a breath stolen away by the wind. No one moves.

The silence rings in my ears. It's more deafening than the sea in a storm.

And I don't want to see details – don't want to note faces twisted in fear or pain, but I do. I'll remember every single one. The mother clutching a child – both still as stone. The old man twisted unnaturally in a heap. He looks child-like in death.

My hand is clenching and unclenching, and I don't know what to do next. I should know. It should make sense to me, but my lower lip is trembling, and thoughts aren't coming through to me clearly.

All our fault. Our fault for coming.

We were contagious after all.

I stumble down the steps, not realizing what I'm doing until my hands are fumbling to rob the dead. Between little shuddering half-sobs, I let them. They're scraping on rock, the nails catching a little, the sound so loud in my ears it must surely alert someone. And then my prize is free – a longsword with a leather-wrapped grip and a sharp blade. She's balanced well. The blade is straight and true.

I try not to look at the face of the nobleman whose sword I've stolen, but I see it anyway and I'm choking for just a moment on my own breath. He's my age. Maybe younger. Face set in fear. And I've taken his sword.

If my shadow guardian was here, he'd tell me to take the scabbard and he'd make comforting sounds while he watched my back. I feel his absence like the loss of my innocence. Feel it in the way a tongue prods at a mouth wound.

Fear still juddering through me, I pluck at the leather belt around the boy's waist, fingers sinking into velvet, trying not to think about how he is still warm. So warm that it feels like he might come to life at any moment.

"Mercy!" screams the macaw, landing suddenly on my shoulder in a flurry of feathers that scrape across my face. I gasp, my heart so far in my throat that it feels like it will choke me.

I can't breathe.

I batt her aside, trying to dislodge her, but her claws only dig deeper into my shoulder. I deserve the pain of it. And something about that sudden sharpness in my flesh stings my eyes and makes it easier to breathe.

Who knows, maybe there really will be mercy someday. Maybe there will even be mercy for me.

I free the belt with a muffled sob, and buckle it around my waist, dropping the cutlass and its scabbard as I fumble the longsword into place. I'm no expert on weaponry, but this blade seems superior to the cutlass, and I know a little better how to use it. Even with my hands shaking like ship bells, I should be able to get the point up.

And with my grave crime committed, I rush back up the steps to the cavernous library – so welcoming only minutes ago in its wealth of books, now like a haven in a raging storm.

My footsteps echo too loudly. Is anyone listening? Will they track me by the sound of my steps?

If I worry about it, I'll end up trapped in a cage of my own making. I force myself forward.

The librarian. Someone needs to wake him. I stumble to his desk and then freeze, hand over his shoulder. What if – ?

I don't finish the thought. His eyes are open.

I draw back with a shudder.

The worst is already here. Well, not the worst. The worst would be if his face cracked in half, and he became a husk for a spirit from the other side of death to take over and steer to evil. That would be the worst.

"Mercy," the macaw whispers as if she realizes we're dealing with something grave now.

"Yes," I agree, "Divine Sovereign have mercy on us all."

"Mercy, mercy." I can hardly tell the difference between her mindless parroting and a prayer.

I leave the librarian where he slumps – I'd like to die on a heap of books, too, if I had to choose my death – and rush into the main hall of the library, picking up my pace to a run as if reaching Stekkan faster will keep me safe and not the other way around.

He's still asleep. I look over my shoulder. Have I been followed? There's no one there. Not a slanting shadow or silhouette. Mercy shifts her weight at my twist. She's heavy. She's real. I can almost see why Stekkan likes her near – it's like a second-by-second reminder that we aren't dead, too.

I hesitate, hand hovering in the air. I don't want to wake him. I don't want him to have to know what I know. Right now, he looks so peaceful. But there's no helping it.

I clench my jaw and lay a hand on his shoulder.

He startles away and the macaw screams, "Over the side! It's over the side!" as she leaps from my shoulder, her droppings splattering across the book I'd been reading on the table.

"Oh. Excrement," Stekkan says, blinking blearily. "On your precious book."

I make a chopping motion through the air. "It's even worse than damaged books."

"Something is worse than that?" he asks, his dimple emerging to wink at me and then disappear again. At my stony expression, his teasing smile fades, and his eyes stray to the sword at my hip. It's all over his face when he realizes I have a new sword. "Show me."

We take the packs – he was clever with them, I realize. They're light and there's only two, plus his lute. I'd feared he'd be extravagant. I still haven't asked how he paid for these things. I think he might have used jewelry he was wearing, or maybe even his family name on credit. I should be thanking him. I should be feeling bad that he had to do that for us.

All of that is blocked out, though, by the city beyond. If he owes someone for what we have, he likely doesn't owe them any longer.

"I sent messages before I came to join you last night," he says breathlessly as I grab the lapel of his canary coat and tug him along.

Where is my Nakuraki? How do I wake him from whatever sleep he's entered to heal? The needing of him leaves me strained inside. My shadow is thinner without him – like it's ashamed to be so empty.

"You sent a messenger after adamantly demanding we don't go home to your country?" I ask, looking nervously at the peaked windows towering high at the end of the hall and at the six peaked doors leading out. I swear I can hear something outside and that can't be good.

"I sent birds, of course. And not just to Ghregoiren, but to my contacts in Cantimar, Haxaluund, Istraverda, and Swordheart. A pigeon can get there faster than we can. Maybe even in time."

I stop short. It's a clever idea.

"I wonder if animals are contagious," I say aloud. "Or birds."

His face is white. "Is it here, then? For certain."

I swallow and turn again. I can't say the words. I don't want to.

"But if it was, we'd hear a panic. You'd have your sword drawn instead of in the sheath."

He's trying to explain it away.

I wish I could.

"Things always seem worse at first glance. Maybe someone's just sick," he says, not even noticing the dead librarian hunched over his desk. There's a flutter of wings and Mercy drops on his shoulder. "Pretty girl."

He ruffles her feathers, and I wish I didn't have to show him this. I wish he could just go back to sleep, and I could keep researching like none of this were real.

"Where did you stable the horses?" I ask him, remembering he'd said he had horses. We'd need them now more than ever.

"At the inn. It's not f – "

His voice trails off as we step out into the sun. Below us, the silent city sprawls, a drunk dead in his sleep. A bear killed in the depths of hibernation. A half-hatched chicken plucked from the egg.

A long moment of silence shrouds all but then the *cloppity-clop* of horses' hooves sends a stab of icy water up my spine. My hand rattles against my sword hilt. Stekkan's hand reaches out and grabs that arm.

"Ilsaletta," he says, choking on the words, his eyes lingering too long on the corpses around us. He shouldn't do that. He can only hurt himself. "Please."

His words are so desperate that I look in his eyes, momentarily distracted from the sound of movement. His lower lip is trembling, and I realize he shaved at some point yesterday. He nicked his chin. What a thing to notice right now.

"Please, Lady Redtide, tell me this wasn't us."

"It wasn't," I say evenly. But where is my guardian? He would be here for this if he realized what was happening. He said he'd never attached himself to a person before – was it possible that what he thought was sleep had trapped him somehow? Something inside my brain starts to scream.

"We were the ones who came here from Salfast," Stekkan says, lines forming on his forehead. "You and me."

"We aren't the only ones," I say, trying to stay calm, trying to stuff the screaming thing deeper into myself. "Jendaya has been here. She tore a page from the last book I opened."

"How do you know it was her?"

The horses are growing closer. I draw the sword from the sheath. Still no Vargaard. It's not just my shadow that is empty without him. It's me.

"Because she stole the page of the book that lists who had the other swords," I say, urgency thick in my voice. "The one that supposedly would tell us how to find a way to stop her."

"You think she came here first. You think she uncovered the gem," he's breathing hard. "You don't think it was us that made this happen. But can you be certain?"

I swallow, taking in the city before us. "Certain enough."

"Then what do we do?" he asks, eyes wide. He lets go of my arm, spinning to look in every direction. "They're all dead. Not even you can protect us, monster hunter. Not even you can stop this."

He's losing control of himself. Unspooling like a loose line in the wind. And I feel like everything is spinning. I've lost Vargaard and I'm going to lose the duke and then it will just be me and a tide-forsaken macaw in the middle of a sea of bodies.

I slap the duke hard across the face at the same moment that I hear Vargaard's voice in my mind.

*"Next time, hold your hand a little flatter and it won't sting so much."*

I gasp in relief. He's here! He's not gone. His very presence fills me up like water poured into a cup.

*"You just had to think my name."*

Had I not thought it before? I turn it over in my mind. Vargaard. Vargaard.

Stekkan's eyes are wide. He swallows, clasping his cheek, and then he nods.

"Yes. Good. Right. I was hysterical."

I nod, but I can't help the tears smarting in my eyes. I blink hard on them. I feel – like something tight was strangling me and now it's gone. I can breathe.

"Don't cry," Stekkan says hurriedly. "I understand. You had to bring me back to my senses."

I want to correct him, but the horses we've been hearing suddenly plunge into view – almost a dozen men surrounding a carriage. They catch sight of us, and the leader holds up a hand drawing them to a stop.

*"While I slept the scourge took the city,"* Vargaard says, assessing the truth faster than I could. *"Princess Jendaya came here instead of to the capital because she wanted access to this library, too. And we're about to meet the first survivors."*

Yes, I agree.

*"Keep your chin up. Don't let them treat you like a child. Use the duke to bolster your assertations if you must, and whatever you do, keep the light to your back so I can hold them off if I have to."*

He's barely done instructing me when the lead horse draws up in front of us. I shift to give Vargaard more shadow in front of me and he's happy to surge into it, man and shadow, muscle and bone and spirit all present, but unseen.

Warmth washes over me at the sight of him. Relief tastes like salt and sunshine.

*"This will take finesse. Be ready for instructions."*

He's all tension and tightness, the muscles in his shadow back tightening as he lifts his shadow sword.

*"Tip of the sword up."*

But I see no smoke or swirling animals made of shadow.

*"Perhaps they're uninfected. But I don't care who looks as if they are good. The priest was good – but he was not for you. And to me,*

*anyone who is not for you is my enemy."*

I can't sustain that level of worship. It isn't right. Not when I'm mortal.

*"Easy now. Be confident. They need to see you do not fear them."*

The rider at the front is an officer of some kind. He has two gold slashes across the breast of his blue coat. A feather in his peaked, rimmed helm. He's Stekkan's age and as polished and shaven and shiny-bright as anyone in the King's own guard.

"Halt there!" he orders.

And I open my mouth to speak but Stekkan moves past me, standing almost protectively in a slightly malevolent-looking swagger.

"Who are you, then?" he drawls and he lets his Ghregoiren accent come to the forefront. "To bark orders at my lady betrothed?"

*"Halls of Felranna!"* Vargaard swears. *"Leave it to the duke to interrupt."*

But I did promise him he could do the talking.

*"He called you his betrothed. I'll wring his neck,"* Vargaard says, and his shadow form is leaning in so close to the duke that his shadowy forehead almost touches Stekkan's. His whole body forms martial lines as if he is about to start a barehanded duel to the death.

I almost think Stekkan can feel him though he can't see him. He shivers slightly, but his dimples never falter as he speaks to the guard on horseback.

"We're the Seamark Hawks, guardians of this city and you

must be a foreigner indeed not to know that and a fool in motley to act as though we are not surrounded by the dead. It is only my kind heart that stops our flight from this place to see to survivors such as yourself."

"Survivors?" I ask.

He touches his helmet in a ghost of a salute, "Survivors from the Wrath of the Gods, m'lady, as I'm sure you can see. We've no room for you in the carriage but if you follow, we'll retrieve a horse from a stable you can ride with us to Swordheart. And you … sir," he says to Stekkan, "can join our rider to Ghregoiren if you like."

"No!" Stekkan says, throwing up a hand.

"Or you may join us in our flight to the capital," the officer agrees.

A head peeks out from the carriage, "Captain! Why are we delayed? We must hurry!"

I'm surprised to realize it's an older woman with a face plain as a farmer's. She doesn't bother sparing a glance for Stekkan or me.

"I care not where you go, captain," Stekkan says, real urgency in his voice, "but I beg you not to send a rider to Ghregoiren. Please, spare her this infection."

"Infection?" the captain says at the same time that the plain-faced woman says, "No disease can take a city in a single night."

I ignore them both. "I care where you go."

*"Easy now. I don't like how the lady is watching you."*

"We're not going to risk keeping word from Ghregoiren over a fancy theory from a stranger dressed like a buccaneer."

"Then take an order from a duke," Stekkan says coolly. "I'm Stekkan Falrune, Duke of Catterail, and I order you to send no runners to my lands."

"Duke of Catterail?" the woman from the coach says, her voice an octave higher.

The guard snorts his words laced with disdain. "Any other orders?"

"Yes," I say mildly. "Don't go to Swordheart. It's not safe. Gather the survivors from this place if you wish – all those who have no colorful smoke around them. Those, you must slay at once. The rest you should put on horses and take to Saltfast."

"Saltfast? The fishing village? You're both mad." The guard's horse stamps as if to emphasize his words.

"It will be safe there," I say, ignoring his tone. "The people of the town are all dead from the illness already, but you can hold up there with your survivors and live off the food stores."

"And what? Trade one tomb for another? Surely you jest." His noble face is twisted up with the thought of it.

"You have enough men here to bury Saltfast," I say quietly, looking at the shaken guards surrounding the carriage.

There are a dozen of them. So few. Somehow, I know this is all that's left of the guard here. There's a roar from somewhere else in the city. The evil are starting to turn. We're all running out of time. And out there somewhere, Jendaya is clutching the stolen page and the stolen sword. I feel like stamping with the impatient horse.

"Do you have enough to bury all of these? Will you live among your own dead?"

In the carriage, a baby starts to cry.

The blunt-faced woman clears her throat, and all eyes turn to her grave face. Her eyes are open pits now, despair filling them.

"Do as the girl suggests, Captain Fairway," she says quietly. "And listen to the duke. The Catterail family have been our friends for these seventeen years past. We trust their word."

She shares a look with Stekkan, and I almost gasp when I realize she must be the Duchess of Seamark. She knows Stekkan. He gives her a mock bow.

"Will you join us, your grace?" she asks, lifting a single brow. The baby is getting louder. Vargaard vibrates like a bow held at full draw as he turns in a circle, looking in every direction at once.

"I think I'll stay with the monster hunter," he says.

To her credit, she doesn't bother questioning that, just waves the captain forward. As they pass, I realize she's the only adult in the carriage. It's packed with children of every age. Every single one that might have been in the castle when the scourge struck, and I shudder when I realize what it means that they are there without their parents and with only this one plain-faced Duchess to care for them. The Duke is not with her. Perhaps he defends his castle.

*"Perhaps she married beneath her quality. People do that, you know,"* Vargaard says, giving the duke a pointed look. *"They do it all the time."*

"We have to hurry if we're going to catch Jendaya," I say aloud.

Stekkan just looks wry as he says. "Do you think she's in the direction of the smoke, or the other direction?"

I follow his gaze and see that inland, black smoke is starting to curl into the sky. Someone had lit the city and it will soon be engulfed in flame.

"Is there any question?" I say with a sigh. "Where there is destruction, there we'll find our noble princess."

There's nothing for it, but to follow – again.

# NAKURAKI

I wake to her – my sun, my dawn.

There's trouble, but there's always trouble. Especially in a world where the Scourge has returned.

Together, we'll conquer it. Or, if we don't, then I will keep her safe from the storm, sheltered from all evil. I'll happily give my future for hers.

I have already offered up my past. Still, I hear the echoes of death groans from the corpses in my soul – the remains of the Vargaards I was before. I do not regret their loss, though the pain of it throbs moment to moment in my heart.

But this time there's something different. She warns me not to worship her.

To stop would feel like an end to breathing.

I try to comprehend the idea of it, but it fills me too full of fear, too rife with agony. Like the idea of walking away from your very own soul. Worse. For I have done that and this would gut me deeper.

Was it the kiss I tried to offer? The comfort I failed to pass on? Was my devotion too naked before her? I will be more careful.

I will be sure she has my loyalty and my constancy with no demand – no, not even a request – for something in return. I will harness myself and rein my heart tightly. I will be like a horse trained to saddle, a dog to the hunt.

But despite my renewed focus, I feel unmoored for I know that while I am exactly the guarding shadow she needs to keep her safe in the chaos of this present day, I cannot help but realize that this duke I hate so much is offering her a different kind of safety. The kind that would last past this single moment and cast a long shadow of safety across her future decades.

And he is not reaching for memories and feeling them slip through his fingers.

I can feel the thrum of thought within me. I can feel the weavings of understanding. I don't want them to fulminate. I don't want to see what I must. Not yet. Not just yet.

Just give me one more day to adore her, to be shadow to her light, to be violence to her innocence.

Just one more day.

# Chapter Seven

"There may be more out here," the duke whispers as he mounts a lovely broad-chested palomino. She whickers under him, tossing her head. She doesn't like the strange rider and the strange smells. She likes Mercy – who is taking up a place on her rump among the saddlebags – even less.

The duke knows horses, I can tell. These are of the quality I'd expect for a duke and fitted with unornamented tack of the highest quality. Were it not for the grooms dead in the stable and a terrible banging and shuffling coming from the inside of the adjoining inn, I would be very pleased.

I gift the duke a very old look.

"I'm only saying there are probably more. Out there somewhere," he says, gesturing with a hand still so graceful that his dismissal looked like a songbird flying away. It must be a strange life to be a duke or duchess. Even stranger to be one in a world where there may be no one left to rule.

*"I wouldn't think much on that right now,"* Vargaard says, but there's a troubled edge to his rumbling mental voice. *"There will be time enough for that when the fighting has passed."*

Time enough for –? I shake my head. He's right. We have

more pressing concerns.

"How many people would you say live in Seamark?" I ask the duke, letting my horse pick his way out of the stable. Oddly, Stekkan chose the doe-eyed palomino mare for himself and a snorting dark bay stallion for me. My stallion is almost a full hand taller than the mare – a horse for a warrior.

"Perhaps as many as twenty thousand. 'Tis a large city," he says as his horse dances unhappily around the poor stable boy. I'd thrown his apron over his face, but there was little else we could do for the lad.

"Then if one man in ten turns to evil, we are looking at an army of thousands," I say grimly.

"Divine Sovereign," Stekkan moans, rolling his eyes at the enormity of it. I feel ill.

*"Unorganized. Unled. That's a different matter than regimented troops."*

An army of two thousand seagulls would kill me with ease, never mind men and women caught up in the passions of the dead.

*"It will be easy enough to slip their noose."*

And the innocents I leave behind? Two thousand of them left to – what? Hide in closets? Stumble from a city filled with the dead – if they live that long.

*"Stop."*

I can feel my chin quivering.

*"Stop."*

He's there suddenly as we exit the stable and the sun bursts out from behind a cloud. He's there streaming out to one side of me, but I turn my back into the sun so I can see him and his shadow hands cup my face – though I can't feel them. His face is drawn in earnest regard.

*"Stop for but a moment and listen, Lady Redtide."*

He shouldn't call me that. For him, I am Ilsaletta.

*"Listen to me, Ilsaletta. You can only fix the broken thing in your hand not the broken things throughout the world. Were you the duchess who rode by, you would care for a dozen children not your own. Were you a woman waking now in this city, finding your family dead, your city in chaos, you would rouse yourself and find your allies and arrange to search for survivors and flee this place, yes?"*

"Yes," I say aloud.

"Yes," Mercy says gravely from behind Stekkan, flapping her wings in a way that makes his mare's eyes roll.

*"And you could do that right now. You could drop everything and hunt for children and the sick who need help."*

I shift nervously because I want to do that.

*"We will, if that's what you choose. But this is the way life rubs at you and blisters the soul. Because you cannot do every good and honorable thing. Sometimes you must choose. Will you stay and help those here who all know – at least in part – what is happening to them? Or will you – the only one who knows everything and wants to stop it – ride with the winds of hell at your back and hurry to warn Swordheart of what occurs?"*

He doesn't need to tell me what will happen if I don't warn them. He doesn't need to remind me that this is only the beginning – only one city among dozens that will fall.

But perhaps Stekkan's message will arrive and warn them.

*"A single pigeon sent out into the sky with a message from a foreign noble."* He says it without inflection or emphasis. But I hear what he means. Pigeons die. Messages get lost.

I will have to be the feather to ride through this city and not be drowned by the "what ifs."

*"Then drift, Ilsaletta. I will anchor you."*

His shadow face is so hard to make out in the light, but I can just catch earnest concern. It's the last emotion I let myself connect to before I take a long breath and close my eyes and I swear I can feel his kiss on my brow as I let myself drift like the feather on the wind, refusing to feel. Refusing to fall back to earth.

I open my eyes and we are already trotting down the street, the duke looking at me nervously.

"Trouble, your grace?" I ask and even to me, my voice is distant.

In my mind, Vargaard is humming to me, a low, somber tune.

"Not your grace. Your … Stekkan. Your Stekkan," he says but the way he's caught up in the words and the way his eyes keep snagging on the dead around us tells me he's just as shaken as I am.

Vargaard's tune stutters, but to my surprise, he doesn't say anything about "my Stekkan."

We're riding toward the fire. We know that's where Jendaya will be. We need a battle plan for when we get there.

"If we find her," I tell Stekkan, "stay behind me."

"Like my life depends on it," he says fervently.

I find myself looking in every shadow, stiffening at every sound. I can't take in the beauty of the city. Where it was overflowing with verdant life yesterday, it's drained of it now as surely as if some deity had doused it with lime.

I tremble a little, but I am the feather. I will not see.

"And what will you be doing?" he asks me, his eyes also skittering over the dead. What must that be like for a healer? To feel the helplessness of a sickness you cannot heal?

"I'll be hunting monsters."

"Of course, you will."

We ride for an hour through the city, and I don't understand why it's so quiet – why no monsters roar to life and attack us. Why no one calls to us for help. We're nearly silent, but even near silence on a horse isn't actual silence. There's still the creaking of tack and the sound of hooves echoing on cobbles and the occasional squawk of Mercy who is sleeping with a head under her wing.

As we finally begin to smell smoke and feel the heat of the flame, we encounter a horse riding toward us at a trot. The rider is dressed like a guard, his eyes wide, a sooty child clutched in his arms. He pulls up in front of us, barely stopping his horse before he's speaking in a rush.

"If you wish to live, either flee or meet us at the western gates. The guard is evacuating all the living we can find, and we'll escort you for safety."

The child stares with hollow eyes, gutting me. What will happen to him?

*"Easy now. He will be well. He is in good hands."*

How can anyone be well after this?

*"Sometimes healing surprises everyone."*

"Your concern is appreciated," Stekkan says gravely, more dukely than I've seen him before. "But we must press onward."

"I beg you no," the guard says. "We've already combed the streets north of here, but the fire is spreading rapidly. We have not the men to stop it. Our guard is down to three men for every ten who were living last night."

Vargaard whistles and I say, "So many?"

The guard frowns but chooses not to ask me why I'm impressed by that. They must have truly been an honorable guard. He is deeply troubled as he reins his horse close to Stekkan. The child starts to shake.

"There's worse than fires that way, m'lord. I saw a man with smoke wreathing him, but he was not ablaze. He pulled my sergeant from his horse not an hour ago and I fear what has become of him." The man clenches his jaw. "And if you think to wait for help, think again. The dovecotes and the streets are littered with messenger doves. The wrath of the Divine Sovereign has taken them, too."

"When was this?" Stekkan asks, alarmed and I clench my fist, too.

"We saw the first fall from the sky when I was eating the evening meal in the barracks courtyard," the guard says, glancing over his shoulder as the fire grows hotter. "I was sent out to investigate. Found the nearest dovecote with every bird dead or dying already and the message-keeper wearing a second smile. It was not an hour later than my bunkmate keeled over dead in the saddle. And after that, well, birds seemed not as important. I must leave you, m'lord. I have my orders. But I beg that you meet us at the western gate."

Stekkan nods noncommittally and is saluted smartly for his trouble. He looks almost martial when he returns the salute. And as the guard rides away, I can't help myself, I'm talking before I realize it.

"Did your family have one of the swords in your keeping, Stekkan?"

He whirls, eyes bright with wariness. "What did you read? I thought you had no clues about the swords."

"I had one," I say, kicking my horse back to a trot. He shies around a body, dancing like he'd like to buck and tossing his head against the smoke rolling out toward us. "The book said one was in Ghregoiren. It mentioned a duke."

I should be watching him as I speak, but I'm not and so it takes me by surprise when I'm taken by the throat. It's all I can do to scream in my mind.

Vargaard! No!

My shadow has slipped between us. The tip of his shadow blade is poised against Stekkan's eyeball, but he shifts subtly to meet my eyes as I claw in a desperate breath. There's a question in them.

No! I try to tell him. Stekkan is – crazy – but not evil.

*"He's going to kill you."* Vargaard sounds panicked.

Not yet. Not yet.

"Promise me," Stekkan growls. "Promise me on your life that

you'll not ride to Ghregoiren."

I've never seen him like this. I've never had my throat crushed so hard. He loosens his grip just enough for me to talk.

*Bat an eyelash and I will take his head. Only let me loose and he will not take in another breath.*

Don't, Vargaard.

"Is this any way to treat your betrothed?" I manage to gasp.

Stekkan lets go of my throat like dropping a snake, like he didn't realize he was holding it at all. His hands shake badly and his face twists in horror.

"What have I done?" he whispers.

He isn't looking at me, which is good, because I'm massaging my throat. I know my eyes are wide. It's like being attacked by a mouse and realizing it almost killed you.

"I don't plan to go to Ghregoiren," I whisper for his benefit. "Though I do need that sword. But I also don't plan to kill you, and I most certainly will if you ever do that again."

*"No,"* Vargaard says. "I *will.*"

I don't correct him. We both know it would be him.

"I'm sorry," Stekkan says, face dark with shame. "I'm so sorry. I don't know what came over me. It's just. It's just … I see these people and I think of my home and my family and I'd do anything to keep this from them."

"Sorry can't mend what's broken," I grumble, but I need to stop speaking. It hurts too much.

"Even if you went there, you could not find the sword you

seek – so please, please don't go." He looks at me out of the side of his eye – afraid to look at me directly but desperate for my assent.

I want to roll my eyes. Instead, I focus on taking slow breaths and try not to think about my throat.

"I am otherwise occupied at the moment," I choke out and kick the horse into a run. He's glad for it. His neck stretches forward, and he settles into an easy lope, avoiding debris on the street as we run.

I thought we could find Jendaya at the heart of the fire but by the time we're close to the flames, it's obvious we won't be able to cross the edge of them. The city burns with abandon, thick black smoke choking the air and the heat nearly unbearable.

My horse shies, fighting the reins and behind me, I hear the cry of "Mercy! Mercy!"

Stekkan is still following me even after that display. I clench my jaw in irritation.

*"To your right! Sword!"*

I draw the sword, on Vargaard's orders, my fingers fumbling. Fires don't produce much light in the middle of the day and my guardian has little to work with. They're on us before I'm ready – bursting out of the rolling black smoke, ash dancing around them like discarded feathers – two broken husks that once were men and a corricle leading them. A grey smoke rat leaps and cavorts around the corricle as he runs. He opens his hand and the rat bursts outward, streaking toward us.

*"Blade up. Brace yourself."*

Vargaard slashes the rat through at the same moment that the rest meet us, one of the husks slamming into my horse. I'm nearly unseated, but the blade I moved at Vargaard's command has passed right through the other husk.

His mouth opens in horror, his breath spicy and revolting. He's so close he's all I can see. I try to pull my sword out, but it's stuck, and I can feel his breath on my face. I shove him back, trying to hold onto the hilt, but he's gripping it, his gaping mouth forming a grin. It's a dead, sickly thing and it curves tremulously like a bow with too strong a draw. He falls at the same moment that I lose my seat.

*"Roll! Tuck the sword under you. Don't stab yourself."*

I obey without thinking and if I hadn't, I'd be dead. My horse is down, rolling just inches from where I would have stood. He would have crushed me. The dead husk is crushed under him and the corricle is dead, too, torn – or slashed – to pieces. I don't stop to tease out the difference.

The last husk abandons his attack on my horse and rushes me.

*"Blade up!"*

But I can't get the blade up. There's something wrong with my arm. I look down to see a dagger stuck in it. Queasiness rushes over me, hot and acidic. It's hard to fight it down.

And then when I do look up, the battle is over. Vargaard cleans his shadow sword on the second man's shirt.

I'm breathing too hard. I can't catch my escaping heart.

My horse scrambles to his feet, eyes rolling in fear, but he doesn't flee. I'm staring at him. He's staring at me, like we both aren't sure if the other is going to attack, too.

*"Easy now. It's over. It's over, Ilsaletta."*

I just want to fall into Vargaard's arms for comfort. I just want everything to be okay. He would make it okay if he could just hold me.

And then, to my utter shock, there are arms around me, and someone is saying, "I'm sorry. I'm so sorry. I'm just so afraid."

My mouth falls open and my sword arm goes limp as I look past a canary shoulder into the stricken eyes of my shadow guard.

He's watching me like I'm stabbing him through the heart. He's watching me with the kind of acceptance you find when life's thread has come to the end, and your eyes are about to close. He closes his eyes and for a moment I see what he knows he can't have – corporeal affection. Love. So much more than a shadow existence. Something in my heart that was holding back feels like it wants to burst.

I step back from Stekkan's embrace.

"I just don't want my land ruined," he says to me, his eyes as black and desperate as the shadowy eyes over his shoulder.

"I understand," I say, and I'm saying it to both of them. "My heart is breaking, too. I'll try not to make it harder than it already is."

*Don't do that for me,* Vargaard says, and he can't tear his eyes from mine, not even when Stekkan leans between us, trying to catch my gaze with his.

"We need to hurry," he says, "that is, if you'll still travel with me."

"Mount up," I say with a sigh. I clean my sword roughly on the back of a dead man's coat and a hot tear shoots down my cheek because I can't be the feather right now.

# NAKURAKI

We're going to destroy her, we two fools. And I'd rather die than do that.

I wanted one more day, but I think that maybe I can't have that. I must hold myself back. I must embrace the shadow. If I don't, she'll stay torn like that, and she won't be able to focus, won't be able to find the comfort she needs where she can get it.

I was born again as hers. I was born to breathe her light. But I will not breathe at *all* if it lessens her. I'll smother happily in this agony of restraint.

And I'll do it a hundred times more if I must.

# Chapter Eight

There's still no sign of Jendaya when we leave the city through the northeast gate. We encounter no one else either – not haggler, nor drover, nor peddler – and the eerie sense that we are alone but surrounded keeps every nerve I have on edge. I am deeply troubled by Stekkan's violent fury. But even more troubled by Vargaard's silences. I do not know what to do, so I hastily bind the dagger wound in my arm, and when the road curves toward Swordheart, I take that road and keep my eyes fixed on the horizon.

I'm startled when Stekkan breaks the silence. His head has hung low since we left the city and other than Mercy's smoke-filled coughs, the pair of them have been as much my shadow as Vargaard is.

We're a pitiful group, smelling strongly of smoke, sweat-streaked, and rumpled. Stekkan paid too much for these clothes and it shows.

"I didn't know what it was," he says, as if he's having a conversation with someone else and I'm only catching bits of it. "We hid away treasures in other nations. You do that if you're smart. Especially if you're in line for the throne. Assassination attempts happen, so you leave fail-safes. Hidey holes. Caches. Surely you can understand that now that you've been forced from your home."

He glances to the side at me. The soot smeared across his face makes him look how I imagine the northern tribes would look when they smear themselves with ash and descend in a ravening horde upon our blue-jacketed soldiers. He has the same wild gleam in the ivory white of his eye.

"Are you talking to *me?*" I ask, but I turn my eyes back to the road. I won't be distracted by the gorgeous hazel of his soot-lined eyes. More importantly, I feel like I'm missing something. Like there's something I just don't see. How do you track a princess? The road is a road – if there's any sign here to look for, it's not clear to me.

In books, there's a clear track and the tracker just knows which one to follow, but where there are tracks – and those spots are limited to damp depressions in the road – there are so many that I don't know which ones to look at and which to ignore. Life is not as simple as it seems to be in books. That annoys me.

"The box was one of the things we hid. In our house in Swordheart," Stekkan is saying. "In case of emergencies. I didn't realize it was one of the seven swords. Not until you began your research and were talking about it. I would have mentioned it if I knew. I just thought it was a family heirloom. We have a lot of those. My ancestors fought a lot of wars." He laughs harshly. "Can you imagine me in a war?"

He sounds guilty but I haven't been concentrating. I've been worried about the lack of birdsong and why the road is so very, very empty. I would have expected merchants on the road, stopped and wondering what to do next. Or refugees fleeing. Or something. Anything.

I pause to listen back to his words in my mind. I feel like I have something caught in my chest.

"Are you telling me, Duke Catterrail," I say very slowly, "that your family *does* have one of the swords – and you're hiding it in Swordheart?"

"Yes," he seems relieved that I've caught on.

"Mercy!" the macaw says with a whistle.

I stare at him for so long that his face burns hot. I wonder if my eyes might fall out of my head. After a moment, I speak through a dry throat.

"Do you know which one?"

"No," he says. "But when we get there, I can give it to you – if you want."

"I think that would be best," I say slowly.

Where is Vargaard? Why is he not commenting on this? I risk a glance at my shadow and see a flicker of him in it, looking ahead with a stony face. The coldness within it pains me. I'm caught between two currents. One that runs viciously hot and one that runs deadly cold.

"It can be your engagement present," Stekkan is saying. "It's customary to give one to your betrothed. The family can't possibly object to that."

"I'm not going to marry you," I say tiredly. "Do we need to talk about the part where you choked me?"

If he was blushing before he's on fire now. "Let's talk about your arm instead. Let me tend it. Your bandage is not stemming the flow of blood."

I look down. He's right.

"*Let him tend your arm,*" Vargaard says. My eyes snap up to his.

I want to ask if he's talking to me now, but I promised not to make things hard for him. Perhaps obedience will be close enough. It hurts worse than any knife wound to know he wants his distance from me.

I draw up my horse into a little stand of trees beside the road. His snort gusts into the sparkling dust in the air. The whole world is a light peach color from the veil of smoke in the air, but it should be safer to stop here than anywhere else. This place can't be seen from the road very easily.

Without speaking, I dismount and offer my arm. Stekkan meets my eyes warily. He should be wary. He's treated me badly today and then tried to make up for it with ridiculous proposals. I'm hot and pained and irritable as a result.

Stekkan is solemn as he tends my wound, as if he realizes any future friendship we might have depends on him doing this well and also on him not attempting to see if the spirit of luck can get him any further in his conquest of my future.

Vargaard is solemn as he watches.

I seem to be the only one especially worried about an entire city consumed overnight by a scourge unleashed upon them by one who ought to have been a friend. I seem to be the only one who is heartbroken over it and still struggling to come to grips with the sheer numbers of the dead.

Well, me and Mercy. She's pacing up and down the rump of Stekkan's horse muttering, "Mercy, mercy, mercy. They all fall down. Mercy, mercy," as the horse rolls its eyes at her. I think the mare is afraid of her feathered companions. I know I am.

"Don't be angry," Stekkan says as he finishes stitching and bandaging. His voice is quiet beside my icy silence. "There is one thing I love – and that is Ghregoiren. Her rolling fields and rippling wheat. Her stallions running free across the striated grass. Her tumbled clouds gathering and dispersing in an endless dance, and her brave, passionate people just wanting to eat and drink and live lives full of wonder and the joy of beauty."

"Admirable, I'm sure," I say, moving the arm gently. He's done a good job. The stitches sting and the arm feels hot and hurt, but it does move. If I have to fight with it, I will. I long for my stolen sword and the icy relief it brings. Would Stekkan's sword lend such gifts?

*"It may lend more than you bargain for. It may offer another Nakuraki."*

I savor Vargaard's voice in my mind – its velvet baritone finds the marrow in my bones and makes it resonate to his particular timbre like water in a glass. I close my eyes for just a moment to hold onto it. He may offer me no touch or kind word right now, but I can have this one thing.

Stekkan is still elaborating on the greatness of his home. I let him. I do not care if Ghregoiren is heaven come down to earth, though I am a little annoyed that I was throttled for the love of it.

I'll never take up a different protector, Vargaard. I will never try to replace you, I say in my mind.

He says nothing in return, and I don't know what to make of that.

"Surely you can understand my desire to protect it," Stekkan is saying. "I will give the last drop of my blood for that land. And yours. And anyone's."

I almost think I'll have to leave these trees without an answer from my shadow when he finally speaks again.

*"To the last drop of my blood, I will defend you. Screaming defiance into the depths."* It's a vow and he pauses before the next part rumbles into my mind, burred with anguish. *"Take what guardians you need. Take every one of them and* live, *book girl. I will stand in your shadow and take every hurt meant for you, but you must not curtail yourself for me. I promised to help you in your heart's work. If that means marrying the duke of wheat fields, let it never be the thought of me that stops you. If it means securing yourself by means of more Nakuraki, let it not be the memory of what might have been a kiss that prevents you. It was wrong of me to take options from you, when all I wanted to do was to give you more – to give you everything."*

My heart feels stuck in my throat. Is that what he thinks has happened? That *he* has limited *me*? I don't deserve this. I will disappoint him.

*"You can't."*

I will. I am mortal. I am made of flaws.

*"Then I am all flaws, too, for I am mortal with you."*

My brow furrows, but I don't have time to ask him what he means because Stekkan has seized my hand.

"You are – of any woman I have ever met – the hardest to woo, but I suppose that challenge shows how rich a reward you are."

I'm arrested enough by his words that it snaps me from the exchange I care about and back to this one.

"This was you wooing me?" I say, lifting a brow. "Telling me you'd spill my blood for your beloved wild horses?"

He frowns. "You are no shrinking violet though you look like a pale, delicate flower, soft and yielding." He shakes himself, realizing, perhaps that he's back on unsteady ground. "But you are a monster hunter, a doer of great deeds, a slayer of terrible foes. Surely you are not offended that I wish to hide not just myself behind you, but all of Ghregoiren?"

He bites his lip charmingly – an effort I'm sure he's used to appealing affect more than once on the ladies of Ghregoiren.

Ah. And now I smile because I prefer it when things make sense. It's not that he has romantic designs on me – other than marriage. He sees me as protection – and I've been promoted in his mind from protection for him, to protection for all he loves. Perhaps he thinks I will be flattered to forever be a guardian for him and his beloved nation and nothing more.

I freeze.

Is that not what I have assumed Vargaard will be for me?

"*It's not the same.*"

It's exactly the same.

I don't even speak. I just give Stekkan a grim look and march back to my horse.

"Yes. Good," Stekkan says, seeming at a loss, despite his words. "You're a woman of action and you'll show me with action. I'm ready to stand in your shadow and watch your back as you fight."

I'd show him an action, certainly. Though possibly not the one he was hoping for.

"*Her shadow is still occupied, Duke.*" But even this comment from Vargaard has none of his usual bite to it. In fact, it almost sounds wistful.

Is he so sad because he really thinks I will marry my popinjay friend Stekkan Falrune, Duke of Catterail? I prod at the idea, hoping he will answer and when he doesn't, worry picks at me like a crow on a bone. He believes I will. He does not want to push me away by criticizing my future husband. Does he think so little of me?

Even that provokes no response.

Vargaard remains silent as we clop down the empty road, turn after miserable turn.

I catalog every waving tree branch, every hoary face seen in the bark, every off lump in the roots or bushes nearby. I'm looking for threats that aren't there. I'm inspecting shadows made only by nature. I'm riddled with the edginess of it so that I jump when a woodpecker breaks through the ash leaves, his wings beating hard and his cry sudden. I bite my lip when a squirrel chitters, flipping his fluffy tail in mock insult. I nearly swallow my own tongue when a hare breaks across the road, his feet silent, black eyes as bright as my own.

The wild animals have returned. So, where have the people gone? Some must have escaped in this direction. The edges of the road are trampled by so many feet I can't read them and the tension inside me runs up my spine like a thread, cinching so tightly I feel like I can barely sit my horse.

And still, Vargaard says nothing.

I have just about decided that maybe I won't make this easy for him after all, that maybe I really will tell him how I'm feeling. And then the unthinkable happens.

I nearly swallow my own throat when a gust of warm wind blows the first note to me. It hovers in the air sharp and sweet as the first snowflake of winter. I'm sure we've triggered a fairy trap or trod upon an ancient curse when I look down and see it is only Stekkan, strumming his lute. He frowns, picks at the wooden tuning pegs, and then tries again.

My mouth falls open as he begins the chords of a famous ballad. He can't be serious. Mercy is singing harmony, her macaw eyes closed in happiness.

Stekkan looks up at me, the rough warm wind tousling his black curls and his smile widens into double dimples and then he says, "If you think it's too dangerous, just give me a signal and I'll stop, but the road's very lonely and I actually entered and won a country festival for lute players once. I went dressed in my body servant's clothing. He didn't mind. I paid him double that week and all the winnings."

"You did," I say, stunned. I feel like I need to look in every direction but other than some birds who have left their trees in affronted indignation, he seems to have no listeners but me.

"It was a piece of my own," he says almost shyly, with a smile that tells me this is his dearest secret and he's just bestowed it on me. "Would you like to hear it?"

*"I sense no enemies about and see no sign. It can't hurt. Perhaps you may find you like the prospect of marrying a musical man. Most women do."*

So, *now* Vargaard shows up. *Now* he tells me all is well. It's almost too much, but I manage a faint nod and a sickly smile and Stekkan begins.

To his credit, he does not play very loudly, and the piece is more of a soft croon than a flamboyant dance. Also, to his credit, he has a good singing voice. He might not be lying about the fair.

I'm hunting the worst monster of all – a princess of the realm

– with nothing but a stolen sword, an irritable stallion, a shadow who wants to marry me off to the first duke he's found for me, and a singing bard who will use me as body armor at the first likely attack.

This is not what I expected when I fled my home.

I try not to let the insanity of the situation dampen my focus. We can't possibly be alone on this road. Princess Jendaya is certainly out there somewhere. I can't afford not to concentrate. Even if Stekkan's song is actually really good and making me want to cry just a bit.

It's a very long day, made longer by the absolute silence from my shadow. By nightfall, we've seen no one, though I've heard more songs than I've heard in all my life before. I find us a reasonably sheltered place to make a camp next to a flowing brook that hides our sounds and offers fresh water. I find it's burbling more comforting than Stekkan's. The brook, at least, does not want my hand in marriage. I'm arranging a long piece of dry wood over a white rock crusted with dark lichen when I finally hear from Vargaard.

*"No fire. They will see."*

I think about what he's saying. It makes sense, but I almost light a fire anyway just to show him he can't just leave and then come back to tell me what to do whenever he feels like it. But why not? Who am I to say he can't do that? He chooses to guard me and live in my shadow but that doesn't make him my slave. It doesn't give me the right to direct him or to make demands.

My cheeks are flaming hotter than any fire when I lay out food for us from what Stekkan bought. He chose well. There are cheese and nuts and dried fruits and a flatbread that still smells fresh even after a day spent in saddlebags. I savor every bite as we eat it together, letting the flavors fill me, and my ears reach out listening for disturbance and my eyes flicker over our surroundings, watching for anything out of place as Stekkan tells me a story of his childhood.

"And then I swept into the room, lily pads in hand, utterly ruining the ambassador's new knee-breeches," he says, laughing to himself.

I can see what he's doing. He watches me as he tells it. It's charmingly self-deprecating. He's trying to form a beginning bond between us.

I manage a wan smile. I don't want self-deprecating stories of royal life. It feels as meaningless as a list of breakfasts eaten.

We tuck our things away, tend the horses, and I take first watch. It's warm, and if it weren't for the horrors I woke to, I would consider it a beautiful night. Birds say their sleepy goodnights in the trees and dusk thickens to the sharpness of night and the moon blooms full as a burnished silver platter.

I wouldn't be able to sleep even if I wanted to. Not with what I have in mind.

I wait until Stekkan's breaths are long and slow and then I act.

I shift to all fours with that bright full moon behind and above me and look down at my dark shadow below me. It takes a heartbeat and then I see the edges of him there. And for just a heartbeat, I'm shocked by the intimacy of this, but the knowledge that from now until always, he'll be in my shadow when I dress and sleep and wash – this close – as close as any lover could ever be.

I don't have time to dwell on it or he'll sense my intentions.

Fast as a whip, I strike, my palm slamming into my shadow

and for just a moment – a bare moment – I feel a man's chest and not a shadow.

He grunts under the violence of my blow.

It's enough to tear a half sob from me, but I won't give in to it. Instead, I press down hard with the palm of my hand and bring the other one up beside it, using the violence of my actions to turn him corporeal.

I lift my chin, ignore the flash-tear that streaks down my cheek, and whisper very distinctly, "You're mine."

"*And what will you do with me?*" He sounds sad, but not angry. I would expect anger from the trap I've set. Instead, it almost feels as if he is savoring this.

"I want to talk to you without you running away." I might start crying if I don't speak quickly.

"*I live in your shadow,*" he says. "*I can no more run from you than you can run from it.*"

"You know what I mean," I whisper hoarsely.

I can't feel his chest under my palms anymore. They've sunk through his shadow chest. I can only feel the granite we're camped on. It leaves an ache in my heart and my palms and I know that he feels it, too, and that's why he has been so quiet, why he's been so grimly accepting of Stekkan's suit.

"*If you want to talk, perhaps we shouldn't do it beside the duke. If he's awake, he'll think you're crazy.*"

"I don't care what he thinks." My voice feels painful in my throat, like it doesn't quite fit.

"*I care,*" Vargaard says.

"You do? You, a glorious Nakuraki, cares what a duke thinks?"

*"I'll not have anyone think less of you, Ilsaletta, no matter how low that man already is."* I swear his shadow hand is trying to brush the hair away from my face.

I let out a long breath – because this is the problem. He worships me – but he's resigned himself to worshipping from afar. And I don't want that. I want to break his curse and free him. I want to slowly, gently, become the kind of friend he'd choose to stay with even without vows or swords or magic. I want to kiss his shadowy lips again.

I stand and walk a little way down the creek – not toward the horses downstream. Mercy would certainly notice that and wake the duke with cries of "Mercy! Mercy!"

I choose to go upstream instead.

I shift to get the moon behind me and I see him slowly curl upward into the shape of a man within my long, silver-limned shadow. It hurts my heart to see him. It feels like it's been longer than an afternoon that he's hidden himself from me.

I could make demands. I could remind him of his vows.

I won't do that.

I would never do that.

"Vargaard," I say carefully. "Do you want to fight alongside me in this coming battle?"

He takes a stilted step forward. *"I chose you over the sword. I chose you over the option of dancing from one Vali to another."*

That's the easy part.

I swallow.

"Have you changed your mind?"

*"You are my dawn and my morning. The bright sun in my celestial sky."*

"I could have used your guidance today, teaching me to read the road. The woods. The way."

He shifts his weight. I can see he's torn but I press on.

"But I'd never force you. You aren't my slave or my bondservant. I want you to be free to make your own choices. To fight the battles you wish. To ignore me if you must."

*"I am Nakuraki. The bonds run deeper than you know."*

"And did you …" I can barely form these words. My arms snake around me, forming a shield and my lips feel too thick to get the words out. I look at my feet. My face feels like the outer layer of skin might burn off. "Did you …?"

*"Yes?"*

"Did you *want* to kiss me on the beach?" I ask and it feels like laying my still-beating heart at his feet.

*"With all my soul."*

And his answer feels like he picked it up and is gently returning it. I swallow. My tongue still feels too thick and now it's hard to see him as more than a wavering shadow because my eyes are glazed over with a layer of saltwater tears.

*"My Ilsaletta. My warrior."* He sounds like he might break as he falls one step closer to me along his inky shadow. Still too far away. Always too far away even in his proximity. *"Don't cry, my greater light."*

"Then why do you withdraw from me?" I ask, looking up

finally and meeting his wincing eye. "Why do you reject me?"

He started shaking his head on the word 'reject' and he's still shaking it.

*"Never. Never that. You will never find anything but welcome from me."*

His shadow hands open and flex as if he wishes he could invite me into their embrace.

"Was that welcome, then, today? When you were silent?"

*"It was space,"* he pleads. *"Space to think. Space without me lurking always just behind you."*

"Vargaard." I say his name and he shivers, closing his eyes for a moment. And I know that feeling. I know it because I feel it when he speaks to me.

"I don't want space," I say, closing the last step between us. "I just want you."

He sighs with his eyes still closed and it's a sigh of longing and want, of surrender and agony. It's all of that in one soft tremble in the air.

I cup my hand around his shadow cheek. I cannot feel it. He cannot feel me. We are – forever – barred from each other. But I don't want him to push us farther apart than that.

I lean in and I hope he opens his eyes in time to see it even if he can't feel it, because my eyes are wide open as I press my lips to where his ought to be with all the purpose and intention and certainty in my heart and for just a moment, I think I feel lips before his eyes spring open, too. And we sit like that for a long moment, neither of us willing to blink.

# CHAPTER NINE

*"And now what?"* he asks me as he swirls around me, his dark baritone vibrating in my mind like a pulse. It's an embrace of sorts, but also not unlike being tucked into an eiderdown. I'm wreathed in shadow, blanketed by darkness.

"Now, you stop trying to marry me off to the duke at every turn."

He's silent at that and I run my hand in a touchless caress along the side of where his face ought to be.

"You don't have to let me kiss you," I say, my voice trembling just a little at the thought that he might ask that of me. "You don't have to be with me on the journey. You can just come out of the shadow when you're willing to come out. I'm no master to you, no bond holder, no queen." I speak faster, sensing he wants to object. "But even if I don't see you except when we are fighting side by side, I'm not marrying someone else. I'm not going to do it."

*"And if your father does not return?"*

Now, it's my turn to say nothing. He knows, then, as I do, that I have no fortune now that Saltfast is ruined and likely looted. With my father gone, I have no means to support myself.

Except for a head full of knowledge, a mouth full of languages, and a sword I'm not very good at wielding.

After a moment he says, *"We can work on the sword."*

I worry at my lip. Perhaps, I will need to be a monster hunter in truth. Perhaps I can earn coin that way – or rather, Vargaard can, and I can spend it on things mortal girls need, like bread and sup.

*"I've failed you."*

"What? No. Of course, not. When have you ever failed me?"

It's I who have failed *him*. He was meant to be the guardian of powerful people enacting deeds of greatness. Instead, he's here with me.

He stills, waiting for me to stop and listen.

*"I've failed you if you think I will not welcome every day with you, gladly throwing myself into your battles, happily sitting with you as you eat your bread and sup. Or whatever it was you were going to spend that coin on."* He seems to almost be smiling from within his flickering shadow. *"I just wanted more for you. Safety. Position. Wealth."*

"And you thought I would get that from a man who hides behind my skirts?"

*"Depending on the positioning of the light, I often find myself behind your skirts."*

I smile at that. Can he see that in the darkness?

*"I see everything."*

Can he see that I'm determined in this course?

*"I wish I could persuade you otherwise – for your own sake. There is so much more to life than spending it lonely on the road, earning your bread from your sword. I want all good things for you."*

"You are the one good thing I never want to lose."

*"You cannot lose me. Not even if you dress in white and speak words with a man in yellow."*

I lost him today, though, and it hurt like a wound.

*"I'll not do that to you again."*

Will he stop trying to force me on the duke, then?

*"You must be careful with him, Ilsaletta. If you travel with him too long, he may actually fall in love with you rather than seeing you as a convenient tool for his own ends."*

I laugh softly. The idea of pretty Stekkan in love with me - him and his lute and his bird and his failed – or possibly too successful – conquest of a princess all turned instead to me is utterly laughable.

*"Sometimes the impossible becomes true."*

I don't reply to that. I let it hang between us and sat silently, soaking in every moment of his shadow wrapped around me, of his presence close enough that it could touch my every thought. I let my pulse race and let little shivers of excitement shiver through my lungs and think about what I will do if the impossible does become true – if Vargaard could be made flesh.

I do not want to stop thinking of it, but eventually, he flickers.

*"Your watch is over, and you need sleep, Ilsaletta."*

I don't want this to end. Not even for sleep. Sleep can be had another time.

*"You won't say that tomorrow morning when I put you through the drills you must practice now if you are to become a monster hunter."*

He's joking, right?

*"Wake Stekkan and take your turn at the blankets."*

"I'm afraid," I whisper. "I'm afraid that if I move, this will be over, and I don't want it to be over."

There's a feeling to him like a still lake just before a duck launches from it. Perhaps he fears the same thing. Nothing in this life is certain.

*"I'm going to be your shadow for a very long time. Get your rest."*

The next morning, he is true to his word. He is still there, wrapped around me – just out of reach, but now out of my heart. I sense him moving in response to my every twitch – a true shadow.

I wake to a cranky Stekken looking despondently at a pot in his hand. Other than his miserable expression, he is like a commissioned painting with the creek rippling behind him and the mist of morning gently rising from all around us.

"No fire?" he asks me bleakly through a yawn.

"No fire," I agree firmly. I am tying my hair back and seeing to little details at Vargaard's guidance.

*For the drills, strip down to the least number of garments you can wear while keeping decent.*

"What are you doing, Ilsaletta Redtide?" Stekkan asks, his tiredness seeming to shed as he watches me.

"Drills," I say sharply.

*"Ignore him. You need to move. I won't work you too hard, but you need to warm up and start to build the strength you need for this blade. Feet shoulder-width apart. Yes, good."*

Stekkan watches me with wide eyes. "I haven't even had my tea, Ilsaletta. Have mercy."

"Mercy! Mercy!" shrieks his macaw.

I'm going to kill that thing before the week is out.

*"A solid plan. She gives our position away. Now, sword out. We'll drill with it in hand. It will help you grow used to the weight and balance."*

Sunrise paints the edges of the mist a swirl of pinks and oranges and golds like dresses at a ball and I move awkwardly into the positions Vargaard guides me in. I wish I could dwell on the almost-feeling of his shadow hands demonstrating where my arms and shoulders ought to be, but the work he puts me through is soon too strenuous to think of anything but the movement.

*"Good,"* Vargaard says when I've finally finished the drill.

My thighs are shaking from the effort and so are my arms. I'm slick with sweat. He takes a sip from his empty tin cup before realizing what he's done and frowning sadly at it.

*"From now on, we do this every morning,"* Vargaard says, and he seems cheerful as I slide my sword back into my scabbard. *"I am cheerful. I like to work."*

"Did you buy any other clothes?" I ask Stekkan.

"Oh. Yes. I did." He turns and rummages through the bags, producing a surprisingly sensible dress with only a little extra lace at the throat and cuffs. It's fitted across the bodice but loose over the legs. I think I can move in it to fight. He's chosen a very feminine periwinkle with cream accents. I'll look the very picture of an innocent lady.

"Thank you," I say gravely, though I wonder how this lace will look doted with blood. It's likely to be in the near future.

I'm behind a stand of wide-leafed plants, dressing hurriedly when I hear Stekkan speak. From the sounds of things, he's saddling the horses. He's surprisingly good with them for a man who has likely had grooms to do this for him all his life.

"I've noticed there are no other travelers. Still."

"It troubles me," I agree, hurriedly shrugging into the dress. I cinch my sword belt over it as well as my utilitarian belt with my pouch of essentials. That's better. My father's coat goes on last of all.

*" The coat makes you conspicuous. "*

It's also the last thing I have of home.

*"Then we'll try to keep it."*

"Do you think that perhaps Princess Jendaya is ahead of us?" Stekkan says. "That perhaps she is gathering up travelers she meets as she goes and bringing them with her?"

"To what end?" I ask, but I've slowed as I think about what he's saying. He makes sense. I hurry to the creek to try to wash out my clothing from yesterday. It's even sootier and more blood-stained than I thought. Maybe it's a good thing Vargaard is not corporeal, or I'd have kissed him in this filth.

*"You did kiss me. Not feeling it doesn't make it not true."*

I feel my face grow hot and I wash the clothing with more

vigor. It's very, very dirty. It needs the extra effort.

"To prevent word of her spreading? To keep hold of anyone who turns into – what did you call those things?"

"Husks," I say. "Or corricles."

"Yes, that. And to kill those who don't turn, as she planned to kill you and me."

Ice running through me makes my stomach feel tight and my throat even tighter.

"Your idea has merit," I choke out.

*"He's likely right. It's the best explanation."*

I come out from behind the bushes to find him in clean clothing, too, his hair straightened and face bright with washing. He's wearing a peacock blue jacket today and a black silk scarf. The macaw preens on his shoulder. But he's also saddled the horses and tidied our camp.

I don't mean to show my surprise, but I must because he says, "See? I can be useful."

"Yes," I agree, frowning. Good ideas. Cleaning the camp. He really is being useful this morning. I look at him furtively, but he's only mounting his horse and whistling to himself. Sometimes I don't know what to make of the man.

We ride out within minutes and all thought of the character of my companion is quickly dismissed when Vargaard whispers to me, *"You're being followed."*

# NAKURAKI

She surprises me. Just when I was resigning myself to losing my light, she comes to me with the sun in her hands and offers it to me with open palms.

And I am not worthy. I will never be worthy.

I am twigs and leaves before limbs of gold.

I am dust and ash before eyes that hold the dawn.

I am wisp and shadow before a warm, beating heart.

And if I could sink into this happiness and live here forever, I would.

But there is the battle to come, and I must be sharper than ever, for I will not be the only one to fight. I must train her hands for battle and her heart to judge. I must train her eyes to see and her ears to hear and I glory in this new work, I revel in the joy of it. I dance, wholehearted, before my every present sun.

And I try not to worry that the memories falling from me like leaves in autumn might be just what she needed to survive.

# Chapter Ten

The air moves around me, and I close my eyes, letting the stallion follow Stekkan's mare. With my eyes closed, everything is clearer. I can smell the horsey scent of my mount, hear the squeak of my leather tack, smell the lemon tang of the oil worked into the straps. A breeze stirs my hair, still tied back from my work, brushing it across my neck and cheeks.

Stekkan hums lightly under his breath. His mare has a distinctive gait. It's easy to pick it out. Thick trees and plants on either side of the road release their sweet scents as the sun warms them. It's shining on my face and hands – just glimmers between the chilly shadows of the trees.

*"Good. Now, listen to what might tell you that you're being followed."*

A squirrel chitters in the trees. But not near, a little behind us.

*"Yes. That's a sign."*

A bird screeches behind us, too. A little too loudly.

*"Now, try it with your eyes open."*

Shouldn't I try to see who is following us? What if it's an enemy? What if he attacks while I'm listening?

*"I'll watch your back. This is a good skill to learn. Now. Eyes open. Listen."*

I block out the horses, and Stekkan and the macaw, and I listen.

We ride like that for an hour before I hear the second set of sounds. The first one is like another companion to me by now. He never gets close enough to see, though I did risk one furtive glance behind us. But he stays close enough that I can track him in my mind. This second one, though, is ahead. And there's more than one.

*"And what do you make of that?"*

I think I see more light ahead. Are we close to a village? Is that a clearing in the trees?

*"Excellent. That is exactly it. And now, I think, you should draw your sword."*

I ease my sword from its sheath as we turn a corner into what had been a village. It's not now. Stekkan chokes almost immediately on the smell, and I want to do the same.

*"Keep your wits about you. Vomit if you must, but you can't lose focus."*

I don't want to take a breath, so I close my eyes for a heartbeat and listen to try to clear my mind. The one following us has stopped just like we stopped. The ones ahead are still moving, getting closer, I think.

As for the village, no one here will ever move again.

*"They're ahead of us by at least a day if it smells. They must not have stopped for the night. And they must have reached this village very quickly after leaving Seamark."*

"But why push their horses so hard when they have days of travel ahead?"

*"That's the question. Pushing that hard means they have somewhere they're going to – a destination. No commander worth his salt would push horses with days of journeying ahead."*

I grip my sword a little tighter. Whoever is coming toward us from the other side of the village is unlikely to be a friend. The people here are either dead where they stood when the scourge hit them, or in the village square. The ones in the square – well, they didn't die of the disease. I don't want to think about how they died, as if acknowledging it will sear it into my brain.

Stekkan vomits dramatically – though perhaps drama is warranted here – and I take the opportunity to guide my horse around his. This might be a fight coming. It's almost certain to be.

My heart kicks up a notch.

*"Stay mounted. Steady now. If we can leave the village first, that's better. Bodies can slip up a horse."*

I feel ill, too. My head is swimming. Oh wait, that's my vision. I want to be the feather. I need to not feel this.

With relief, I find that place where I don't feel, where I just act. I grab Stekkan's reins, not relenting when he says, "I'm fine." He doesn't sound fine. I don't feel fine.

I guide his horse out of the village and I'm glad I do. He's clinging to the pommel. He vomits twice more as we ride but I don't stop to let him do it in peace. The less we see of what has been done here, the better. He's lucky. It's hard to see anything when you're spilling your breakfast all over the ground.

If there are more villages, we'll ride around.

*"Yes. Good plan."*

Vargaard seems grim.

*"They're close. Do you hear?"*

I hear their horses' feet on the hard road as we clear the village and even knowing that they're coming, I'm not ready as they break into sight.

It's a pair of men in royal guard uniforms. They are tidy and oiled and calm. Which, all by itself, is insanity given what we've just ridden through and given what they can see behind us. They ought to be puking like Stekkan or empty-eyed like me.

*"Listen carefully. These men mean you harm."*

I could see that much.

*"And their fellow is close behind us now, within sight. Don't look."*

I don't look, but I grip the sword a little tighter, studying the faces before me as the stallion dances nervously.

*"Give the duke his reins."*

I thrust them towards him wordlessly and to my relief, I feel him take them.

I'm riveted by the faces of my opponents. Two men. One Stekkan's age. One in his forties. Their mouths are set in grim lines. I don't like the look of determination in their eyes. Their hands are on their hilts and when the older one speaks his friendly tone is completely at odds with his tight movements.

"Halt, in the name of the king!"

*"You won't like this next part."*

My horse is nervous and I'm even more nervous about fighting from his back. We didn't practice that.

Will these men attack? I don't see much smoke around them. And they are claiming to belong to the king – not the princess – the king. I'm no traitor. Just the thought of treachery makes my hands sweat.

*"I need you to do exactly as I say."*

I lick my lips. I'm ready.

*"You aren't but you must act. Kick your horse further in front of the duke's."*

I obey immediately even though there doesn't seem to be room.

"Halt!"

I have not halted. We're still trotting forward. I'm only horse lengths away.

*"Whatever you do, keep control of the stallion and don't let him throw you."*

Throw me? A worm of worry is crawling in my belly.

*"To the left, now!"*

I dance the horse to the left as we meet them on the path and Vargaard launches out, corporeal in this moment as he leaps for the saddle behind the nearest rider. He lands on his feet like a cat. His shadow blade is out in less than a second and he jams it into the neck of the soldier.

I gasp, but no, I don't have time to be shocked. My horse is dancing again, and then my enemy's horse collides into mine and it's all I can do to keep my seat.

Behind me, Stekkan *does* have time to be shocked. Between his curses and the macaw's imitations of them, we can be heard for miles.

"In the name of the king!" the other man yells, charging toward Stekkan.

I shake off the dying rider who is trying to cling to my horse's reins, slamming my hilt on his knuckles until he lets go. I miss the last one and hit the stallion. He rears.

I can only hold on with one hand and I do, my breath sawing out of me, blood in my mouth from where I bit my tongue. I'm trembling and it hardly matters because the stallion is trembling, too. The ground comes up and hits us like a boat on a troubled sea, jarring my teeth together. I grasp for the reins I lost, snatch them up, and tug him to the side to wheel him, but he doesn't trust me now and he's mad.

He snorts and tugs in a full circle so that all I see is a snatch of Stekkan's wide eyes, his bird screaming, "Mercy! Mercy!" and then Vargaard leaps as my shadow crosses the second guard and he yanks him from the back of his wild-eyed mount and stabs him in the throat.

I don't watch his choking death. Instead, I gasp in a long breath, my own eyes nearly as wide as those of the fleeing horse and I'm about to sigh in relief but it's too soon.

The man who had been following us has Stekkan by the back of the neck. He puts the knife to the duke's throat and his grin is terrible.

But more terrible still is the orange smoke seeping between his teeth as he says, "And what do we have here?"

# CHAPTER ELEVEN

Stekkan's horse dances to the side but the man keeps a tight hold on the duke so that he's stretched out, lower body still clinging to the saddle, upper body held in an unwanted embrace. To my surprise, Stekkan doesn't look terrified. His expression is one of intense concentration.

*"Chin up. Pretend this doesn't bother you."*

I raise my chin.

"You've been following us," I say it without even a shake to my voice and I'm proud of that.

Stekkan's horse eases slowly back toward him. That's what he was concentrating on. Clever.

*"Edge your horse to the side so my shadow can reach him."*

I start to move and the man holding Stekkan clicks his tongue.

"None of that," he says in a rough voice, the smoke curling from his mouth and wrapping up around his head. It's a smoke viper, I realize, which makes him one of the dangerous ones – a corricle and not just a husk. The spirit that tried to possess him is now controlled *by* him. It tangles down from his head and swirls around Stekkan's green face. The duke's eyes dart to me, as if pleading for salvation. Now that his horse is where he wants it, the fear is leaking through again. "Move and this man is dead."

*"We'll have to rush him. We can't let him take us anywhere."*

But if we rush him, then the duke is dead. I grit my teeth. I didn't ask Stekkan to follow me, but I don't want him dead, either.

"Consider yourselves prisoners of Princess Jendaya," the man with the snake says. "Drop your sword."

My hand flexes around my sword, but before I make a move, Mercy leaps up from her place on Stekkan's mare, screaming "Mercy! Mercy! Mercy!" as she lunges for the smoke snake.

It's all the distraction I need. I kick my horse forward and to the side and like an arrow loosed from a bow, Vargaard darts forward.

*"Stay out of this. I have it."*

But this time I ignore his order, plunging toward the fray. Stekkan's captor is beating at Mercy, but to do that, he's had to lower his dagger. His snake bursts into clouds of smoke wherever the bird attacks and then it turns, wrapping around her as her cries fade into a strangled squawk.

Stekkan claws toward her, begins to topple, and I catch him at the same moment that Vargaard pulls his captor to the ground.

I lose track of what happens next. My hands are too full of bright blue cloth and ambergris perfume. Stekkan is surprisingly muscled under his jacket for a man who seems to never lift a finger for more than lute playing. His breath saws as he fights with me to regain his balance. By the time he's settled back into his saddle, it's over. The man who attacked us is dead, sprawling on the ground, his limbs at impossible angles. Vargaard looks up from where he crouches over our enemy, a grim expression etching his shadow face.

I'm about to speak when Mercy – rather the worse for wear – launches up with a shriek and a rain of crumpled feathers, flaps awkwardly to Stekkan's lap, lands, and then promptly turns in a circle and flops limply across his legs.

"Mercy," he whispers, looking stunned as he inspects her feathered body.

I leave him to tend the bird and to figure out how to get that stunned look off his face. I have bigger worries than dramatic macaws.

With all three men dead, I have no idea who they are or how to avoid further detection.

*"Search the bodies. To do that, you'd usually look for amulets or crests to identify who they work for, but the man was clear that he worked for the princess and he came to the aid of the others, so they are likely together."*

That seems reasonable.

*"Dismount and check belt pouches. We have only moments, but information is important."*

I dismount, surprised that I'm trembling. How can this little scrap of violence still shake me when I've been through so much already?

*"Did you think to grow used to killing? I hope you never do."*

My stallion is just as unnerved as I am, so I settle him with gentle hands and keep a firm hold on him as I check the bodies. Our trust is still tenuous. He hasn't forgotten my accidental strike.

Our fallen enemies' belt pouches produce nothing out of the ordinary. Flints, knives, bits of string, coins – which I leave be. I don't feel right plundering them of more than their lives.

Wait. The coin is Ghregoiren. That's unusual. And they wear no crests. But I suppose anyone could carry Ghregoiren coin.

*"Hmm."*

I'm surprised by these first two. They show no signs of being husks or corricles. Is it possible that they were good men?

*"Doubtful. I would think it means they are newly infected."*

And if that were true then they have only recently met Princess Jendaya and those who work for her – or they haven't met them at all.

*"And yet they worked in turn with the man following you."*

Or he seized the opportunity to grab us when he saw we were vulnerable.

My eyes meet Vargaard's in understanding. There's a force ahead of us. That's clear now. They may or may not be working with the princess. They may or may not be from the duke's homeland. But these two are on patrol coming from that force. Which means an encampment.

Is it possible that this patrol was coming to the village for the first time? Was it possible that they thought *we* caused the chaos and death behind us?

Could we have killed innocents? I feel ill. I need a moment. Why does my breath hitch so hard?

I didn't even try to stop Vargaard.

*"You couldn't have stopped me. I know trouble when I see it. You,*

*my Vali, my girl of books and salt shores, you are my heart, and I will never let anyone touch you – no matter how innocent they may be of other crimes."*

What if we were wrong?

*"We weren't. I am confident of that. You must not take on every burden you find. No one can carry them all."*

I can't help it. This cuts at me with a thousand small cuts and every one of them stings.

*"I am not worthy to dwell in your shadow, Vali."*

That's not true – but I can't argue it with him when I am hard-pressed to even think. I will never know if we committed a travesty, but I do know that I can't afford to stay on the road. We must travel more carefully. There can't be any lute playing in our future.

*"That's always a good rule to follow."*

I mount again and turn to Stekkan. He is carefully bandaging one of Mercy's wings. The macaw has recovered enough to shoot me a slit-eyed glare. That's right, Mercy, I didn't jump to your defense, though I did appreciate the help.

*"It would be better if the bird flew away. We would have found another opening in the fight, and she is too visible."*

So is the duke.

*"I didn't want to be the one to say that. We have to move. There will be others."*

"We need to leave," I tell Stekkan.

He doesn't answer but his hands don't stop moving over Mercy's wing.

I reach for his reins and his hand shoots out to stop me and now he looks at me.

"When does it end?" he asks me, hollow and full all at once like a pitcher of tears.

"When does what end?"

*"Oh, depths of the five hells, not now! We do not have time for this."*

Stekkan looks up at me, his face drawn. "They hurt my bird. They killed those villagers."

He pauses to swallow heavily.

I don't point out that we don't know for sure if it was our attackers who killed them. That they might even be his countrymen. He doesn't look like a man who wants to quibble over details.

"I can't go home, or I'll spread it," he continues, hopelessly, "but every step takes me deeper into violence. It's breaking me, Ilsaletta. I'm not strong like you are."

He looks younger than his twenty-eight years. Younger than me. I bite back a sigh. I am not good with children and I'm not sure I'm good with Stekkan either.

*"Tell him this is not the time for a mental breakdown. I've watched men's bowels loosen as the enemy approaches. I've watched them drop their weapons and flee, clutching their heads as if they can block out the cries of their pursuers. I've seen strong warriors melt like wax and curl into balls among the grass like fawns left by their mothers. That's the duke right now. We cannot let him make us the same. This kind of thinking is infectious."*

"We have to go," I say as gently as I can. "Let me lead your horse."

Stekkan looks stubborn for a moment. "You go be a hero. I'm not going a step further. I won't make things worse for anyone, but I'm done with heroics. Do you hear me? Done."

*"Good. We can move faster without him."*

And he'll be safer on his own, too.

I think.

Maybe.

"You'll turn around and go back to Saltfast?" I ask. It makes the most sense if he wants to be safe. He knows that there are good people headed there.

He says nothing.

I can't afford to sit and wait. Not here on the road where we're vulnerable. I look up and down the road. There isn't any movement but that doesn't mean there aren't more enemies out there. I can feel them creeping down on me like insects as dusk falls.

"You can't stay here. It isn't safe." I'm worried about him, too. I feel responsible for him.

*"You aren't."*

Still nothing from the duke.

*"We have to hurry. There will be more. And if you want to reach Swordheart before them, we have no time to lose."*

I clear my throat. I don't know how to say "you made this horror less horrible." But I should say something as a goodbye.

I settle on, "Thank you, Stekkan Falrune, Duke of Catterail. I am in your debt for the help you've offered me these past days."

He doesn't look up.

*"Come on, book girl, we must move."*

I double-check that I have all my own saddlebags – I can't afford to lose the maps – and then with a sigh, I wheel my horse and crash into the forest beside the road. I'll need to move hard and fast to put distance between myself and this village.

Branches break as I forge my way into the woods and off the road. I'll miss the duke and his lute and bird. I'm surprised by how sharply I feel his unsaid goodbye.

Maybe I should have offered something more. But I didn't have more to give.

Long minutes pass and I try to focus as we weave between trees and thick-fronded plants. I have enough on my mind. I can't waste it worrying about dukes with enemies ahead.

I do know I feel a little more lost without him there.

*"He's following you."*

I glance over my shoulder. Stekkan's head is down as he plunges through the trees, the bird hugged to his chest. And I don't know if I should feel bad for him because he looks so helpless, or angry at him for not making sense, or suspicious because it was his country's coins in those pouches and now he's following me in a way that can only be thought of as utterly incriminating. Or maybe I should just be relieved because I didn't want to lose my friend when I was growing used to having him with me.

I rein in my horse and try to control the hot clouds in my head. Irritation will not help. Guilt will not help. I need to remember that he's a duke and a doctor and not used to hard travel and tragedy.

*"And neither are you and yet you keep pressing on."*

I feel my cheeks heat and I can't help it when my frustration grows even hotter at the sound of his horse walking so loudly through the trees. He's going to bring anyone in a league toward us.

*"You could leave him here. I could easily help you slip away."*

I won't do that. I feel responsible for him – even if his sudden whiplash of intentions has left me feeling just as confused. Besides, he's helped me more than once.

He reins his horse beside me and when he finally looks up there's betrayal in his eyes.

"You left me," he says.

"You're being ridiculous." I try to keep my tone calm. It's about as easy to do as fighting monsters – not easy at all.

"I could have been killed."

"And yet, here you are." Perhaps it's still more acidic than I meant it to be. "I thought you were going to go back to safety."

"I thought you were going to keep me safe," he mutters. His lower lip is thrust out.

I don't like this side of him. It reminds me of when we first met. Worse, I feel outside of my expertise. I am not used to soothing feelings or nursing bruised hearts. Especially not when I don't know what's harmed them. I try for the obvious.

"I'm sorry about Mercy," I say.

"She may never fly again," he says with a trembling lip, his wide hazel eyes bright with emotion. But the bird is having none of it.

"Mercy, mercy," she grumbles, squirming out of his grip and fluttering into the air despite the bandage to land on his shoulder. She spits at me – really spits – and then jams her head under her wing. Well. We're all cheerful then, aren't we?

I take a long breath. I'm not good at apologizing.

*"Why are you apologizing? You've done nothing wrong. Were you a man, you would have left him back in Saltfast unless he was paying you a fat gold purse or was an emissary of your god."*

Even so. I don't want to ride with an angry companion.

"You'll be as safe with me as anywhere else now that the scourge is spreading," I say, sticking to facts. "And I'm still pressing on as hard as I can for Swordheart. Do you want to join me again?"

"I thought you'd come back for me. Or that you wouldn't leave," he says which is *not* an answer.

"I'm riding on," I say as evenly as I can. I *do not* understand what he wants from me at all. "And you're welcome to come."

And I face forward and kick the stallion into a walk again. I don't want to look back. I know he's following by the too-loud sounds of his horse.

"I forgive you," he announces eventually. "And I will still marry you."

It's all I can do not to put my hand over my eyes. In my mind, Vargaard is laughing. He can keep that to himself. There is nothing funny about this at all.

# Chapter Twelve

Even following Vargaard's commands, I do not feel very confident in my abilities as we slink between the trees along the road. We do not speak, even the duke realizing that we're in danger here. I spend the time I might have spent talking deep in worry. How well do I really know Stekkan? Is his nation allied with Jendaya? Would he betray me to her if he finds out where his country's loyalties lie?

*"Worry steals your watchfulness. Keep focused,"* is Vargaard's only opinion on the matter. His voice – thick as molasses and just as darkly rich has a reassuring quality.

We are not moving silently – a fact that sets buzzing flies of worry inside my mind. The macaw mutters constantly to herself even with her head under her wing. Stekkan's horse seems bent on stepping on every dry twig ever made and even my stallion huffs far too loudly.

*"It's in your mind. You're no louder than any other group of novice foresters trying to be silent."*

Worse, it reminds me of riding the high road with Stekkan. Of finding the priest. I do not like it. I do not like the feeling of exposure it gives me even as the branches around us press in. I see figures waiting for us in every shadow. Ghosts of my mind and no more, and yet they set my teeth on edge.

We kick up a squawking raven and I nearly draw my sword.

*"Deep breaths. I haven't seen any scouts. We are safe enough for now."*

I hear the camp before I see it – a shock given how badly we stalk through the woods. There's a rushing like wind in the trees and it takes a while before I realize that it's voices. When we finally peek out from a tree-encrusted ridge of yellow rock, my heart freezes in my chest. There are armies in the valley below where the road cuts through – three of them. One flies the banners of Ghreghoiren. One the banners of Cragspear. One more banner I've never seen before. It's a green diamond on a black field. I can guess who has made that her banner.

I feel as though a snake is creeping up my spine. Fear pins me in place as easily as a fly pinned to a board.

*"Stay very still. Watch and think. I agree with you that the green diamond must represent the princess. Why does she fly her own banner?"*

She must want to carve her own nation.

*"Will she not inherit this one?"*

She will. It's hers the moment her father stops breathing.

*"A symbol then? A clear sign of what is to come?"*

The thought of that makes me ill. I still haven't been able to think of that village without waves of nausea crashing over me. I do everything I can to only think of Seamark as it was before I entered the library and not as it was when I left. I don't dare think about children or mothers with babies or the helpless. I don't dare think about what survivors must do. I don't dare think about how slim their chances of survival are without a Vargaard to rescue them.

*"Ilsaletta."* Vargaard's voice is like a whipcrack. It snaps me back to right now and I saw in a breath and force myself to float for a moment. I am the feather. I drift over this like a feather on the wind. I do not feel the breeze below. I concentrate on my horse's warmth beneath my legs. Think on how he seems to be taking to me. Feel the breeze on my cheeks and the hot sun where it is searing just one of my shoulders and after a moment I can breathe again.

*"Now that you are calm, look."*

The camps are not what I'd expect. I've seen diagrams of military camps in my father's books. They're shown as tidy rows of tents with large common pavilions or as clusters around shared fires. This camp is laid out differently. There are pickets for the horses, certainly. A guard set around the camp. Cookfires at the center, jakes dug to one side. These things are what I would think to see.

The three banners – that's something I didn't think to see. They are flying over three clusters of tents – the Greghoiren one being the closest to us and Jendaya's the farthest. These three groups are distinct, almost as if someone has drawn a line between each one and no one may pass. Apart from all three camps are another set of tents – a rough tumble of canvas and people that is nothing like the military precision of the three bannered groups. And beside that tumble, a large number of men are digging holes.

It takes me a moment to realize that the holes are graves.

It takes another moment to notice the men with barrows hauling lumps of cloth from the tumbled tents towards the holes.

The dead, I realize, and I shouldn't be shocked anymore and yet I am.

Two lines of soldiers have formed at the edges of the Ghregoiren and Cragspear camps and now they begin to march into the tumbled-down tent area.

"*Well,*" Vargaard says grimly, flickering just beside me, a faint shadow in the afternoon sun. "*Now we know what she is doing. Creating an army.*"

Creating? It looks like she has three already.

"*She's filtering them slowly into the infected ranks and sifting out what remains.*"

The breath sticks in my throat. That's exactly what she's doing. I look more carefully at the army beneath the green diamond banner. It's swelling at the seams. That's where they go when they've turned, isn't it? And that's where they've taken those who survived the infection from the city and the village – those evil enough to be husks.

"*I think so. I think it explains why the road was so quiet. There were other travelers, but she found them before we did.*"

What does she tell them? How does she explain what she's sending them into when so many of them end up dead after? And what is happening to those who neither die nor turn?

"*Likely she tells them she is offering them the change of power beyond what they can imagine. That's enough for most men. Especially soldiers, whose lives are determined by their skills. As to what they do with those who survive and don't turn – well, it's always easy to dig more graves. At this rate, she'll have filtered the whole camp through by tomorrow.*"

I'm not fast enough. I'll never be fast enough. But there's still time. I can skirt this army, riding through the woods and get back onto the main road on the other side and then ride like the wind for Swordheart. When the king hears of this, he will know what to do.

*"And will he hear you when you speak against his own daughter?"*

He has only to send scouts to look for himself. But we need not worry about that now. One worry at a time.

*"The duke would be handy when it comes to telling the people in power what is happening."*

As if he hears his name, Stekkan edges his mare up to beside my stallion. He looks up at me and whispers, "That's Ghregoiren's banner."

I nod.

"They shouldn't be here."

I nod again. No one should be here. Not even us.

"You don't understand, Ilsaletta," he says, scratching at the light beard coming in and studying the camp. "They're my people. My responsibility. I need to go down there and warn them."

All traces of the man who sulked because I didn't go back to get him when he was upset are gone. His eyes narrow with determination and his mouth forms a firm line. I like this Stekkan. But he's still wrong.

"And the dead bodies they are throwing into those graves aren't warning enough? The survivors leaking colored smoke and cracking down the middle aren't enough warning?" My words are hard, but my tone is gentle and for a second time I lay a hand on his arm.

He startles at my touch, looking from it to my face.

"It will be okay, your grace," I say, choosing his title deliberately. It's the duke in him that cares for his people. The duke in him that is worried. "We'll warn the king, and he will put a stop to this."

He's already shaking his head. "You don't understand. All my decisions, every one of them, have been to keep this scourge from the shores of Ghregoiren. But where do you think the men under that banner will go? They will go there next. They will ravage my homeland and all my precautions will be for nothing."

"We are three days journey from Swordheart, your grace," I whisper urgently.

I'm worried about the fire in his eyes. He's going to march right down there and start commanding them, I just know it. And they'll kill him on sight.

*"He does have that look. You need to find a way to stop him. He'll be captured and the moment he is, he'll tell them everything about you."*

And also, I like Stekkan and don't want him dead.

*"His utility outweighs his expense."*

That's high praise coming from Vargaard.

"We are four days from the Ghregoiren border," I remind him. "If we hurry around the army, we can get back on the road and press on. We can send another pigeon from the capital to your homeland and even a messenger with strict instructions to deliver only a letter and avoid all contact. We can warn your people before this army gets to them, but we need to go now."

"And what if they break camp and march out today?" he asks

me, his whisper urgent. "What if they reach Ghregoiren before my message can?"

"It's a risk we'll have to take," I say but I don't like how his arm is thrumming under my palm. I don't like that look in his eye. "You can save no one if you're dead."

He looks down and then looks up again and I don't like how grim his eyes are or how I think I see an unshed tear in them.

"I am sorry, my betrothed, but my duty here is clear. Be safe and well and may we meet again."

"*Stop him!*" Vargaard urges but though I lunge for Stekkan, he's already slipping from my grasp. He heels his horse, and she breaks the cover of the trees, plunging toward that death camp below. Noble idiot.

Even over my bitter curses, I can hear the macaw screaming, "Mercy! Mercy!"

"*Get a hold on yourself. Quick now.*" Vargaard's words are urgent. "*As soon as they realize who he is they will trace his steps to this place. We must melt into the trees.*"

I can't do that. I have to go after him.

"*I am Nakuraki. No longer of mortal planes but the plains of spirit, dedicated to war and death, but I cannot defeat an entire army on my own. We do not have the numbers here. Our only options are to hide or to flee.*"

I swallow and my pulse is so loud in my head that I can't even hear my own whispered curses. With difficulty, I say, "Tell me what to do."

"*Turn the stallion. We must retrace our steps until we can find a way to leave our trail without pointing out where we went. The next few hours are key to whether we will be discovered."*

And Stekkan?

*"Once you're safe we can talk. Perhaps you want to sneak back and try to save him. Perhaps you'd rather press on and save the rest of your land. The choice is yours."*

And with that we press on hard, retracing our steps, then carefully leaving that path for another while trying not to leave a trace. I follow Vargaard's instructions to the tiniest detail, but this is a new skill for me. I must concentrate hard to get it right. Fortunately. Because if I had any thought to spare, I'd be worrying about Stekkan and what manner of torture he might be finding in the camps of his people.

# Chapter Thirteen

I am nearly free when I make my first error. I've been carefully circling the camped armies, avoiding detection by patrols and carefully feathering through the grasping branches and treacherous ground. This is not easy to do with a nervous stallion. Even less easy to do with an uneasy rider. I can see a clearing ahead, separate from the camp, and the relief that fills me is so strong I nearly sag. We've found the road again.

*"No, I don't think that is the road."*

But I can see it and after what feels like hours of combing my way through the woods, I was starting to think I was lost.

*"We are not lost. It has not been many hours. And the shape of that clearing is wrong. You need to stay back. We'll watch carefully from here."*

My stallion snorts and I put an absent hand on his nose to comfort him. I've been on foot for the last hour leading him through the forest. It's not fit for riding.

*"Keep your footsteps in my shadow."*

That's what I've been doing all along, carefully following him step by step.

I can see nothing except that there's an opening. If the shape of it is wrong somehow, it eludes me. The woods here are crisp and beautiful, every line standing in the stark contrast of the late afternoon sun. The heat begins to leech away as evening approaches, and the sun-drowned plants release their warmth back to the tender breeze.

Were we not a short way from a camp of monsters, of the dead and dying, of my greatest enemy and my lost friend, then I could sink into the beauty of this place.

I take another wary step forward.

*"I want you to skirt to the right and edge around that fallen tree. If this is the road, that track will run parallel to it."*

And if it is not the road?

*"Then we will have lost a little time."*

I don't want to lose more time. I just want to see for myself if the road is there.

*"I do not advise it."* But despite his words, he is beside me, flickering in his faint, faint shadow form but leaning forward like a dog pointing toward the hunt as we strain to see through the trees.

Just one step won't hurt.

I take a step forward, careful to be silent, all my weight in the ball of the foot. Behind me, the stallion snorts again. He's picking up on my caution perhaps.

I still can't see the road. A worm of worry crawls in my belly.

And then the skittish stallion nickers.

I turn, fear blossoming in my chest. Has anyone heard that?

*"Patrol. In the trees. Stay still. Do not move a hair."*

I am utter stillness. I do not move. I barely dare to breathe. I feel – more than ever before – a sense that Vargaard is right there with me, wrapped around me, protecting me while still more gossamer than the wind.

*"Easy now – gentle breath. I hide you in my shadow."*

I take a breath. The fear tangles in my belly but I must not let it win or I will bolt.

*"One more breath. Gently. Eyes in the distance. Look to a point as far as you can see."*

Is that where the patrol is?

*"No, but it will ease the nausea of fear that runs hard in your veins."*

I do as I am bid. After what feels like far too long, Vargaard relaxes.

*"He has passed. But now we know the clearing ahead is not just a road. Perhaps they have put up a pavilion there."*

So far from the camp?

*"Perhaps. It's common to put a well-guarded command tent a little way from your troops if you're in friendly territory. Some of what military leaders do is best kept from the eyes of the regular soldiers – or so it is thought."*

Then we will have to skirt that, too.

*"We will, and it seems it lies directly beside the road we must take to the north."*

It is easier to decide than it is to do, for the earth rises in a sharp bluff and as we try to skirt the camp the edge of the crumbling bluff runs closer and closer to the road.

*"The road runs between the cliffs ahead,"* Vargaard tells me though I can see it from where we are huddled.

Already, our place is precarious, and I am grateful that the stallion has remained mostly quiet. There's a wind blowing through the trees strong enough to disguise his occasional missteps – and mine. But even so, the pickets for the command horses are close.

We are right on the edge of forest and road. Their pavilion spreads before us and the road just past it. If we try to swing back south, we will end up traveling between the command tent and the main body of the army – a plan that can only end in our discovery. We cannot go deeper into the woods without spending days wandering, looking for another way around the rising bluffs. While we would likely succeed in finding a path, we would lose any chance of warning Swordheart.

*"I will remind you that you can still walk away from this. I can guide you somewhere far from this conflict where you will be safe until it passes."*

But that has never been an option for me. What is safety if I live it in the sure knowledge that someone else suffers because I wouldn't try to save them?

Which leaves only this option – skirting the camp to the north and east and squeezing between the bluffs and the command tent. There is barely the width of a horse between them, and I do not like it at all. Perhaps, I should leave the stallion at the pickets and go on alone.

*"You cannot hope to race this army on foot and without supplies and you cannot carry the saddlebags and go faster than they. If you're*

*set on this course, you need the horse."*

I swallow. I can see soldiers guarding the tent from where I hide in the shadows. I can see them moving about their tasks or standing stiff and formal on the other side of the pavilion. The wind snatches their voices – a wind worse down here between the bluffs on either side of the road.

*"The landscape shapes the wind, drawing it between the rocky walls,"* Vargaard is saying. But suddenly, I do hear something – the faintest edge of a scream. *"We move. Now. While the scream distracts them. Ease in behind the pavilion."*

I cannot seem to move my feet. I'm going to be caught.

*"Deep breaths. Do you see me in the shift of the shadows?"*

My shadow is the faintest puddle around my feet and toward the camp. It's barely there at all.

*"Cling to my shadow. I am with you, and I am between you and your enemy whether you can see it or not."*

I swallow against my dry throat and hold onto the idea of that, creeping with him along the edge of the pavilion. We are at the midway point where the pavilion swells out the farthest, creeping, creeping.

And suddenly the wind dies.

I want to curse.

I don't dare do so much as breathe.

And then I hear it.

"Mercy," someone in the tent says. My heart seizes in my chest. No, not someone. Some*thing* because it continues, "Mercy! Mercy! See how they fall!"

I breathe so hard I feel like spots are dancing across my eyes. Stekkan must be in there! But why would they have brought him here to this out-of-the-way command pavilion?

And what about that scream?

*"Don't think of it. He is no longer your responsibility."*

There is low murmuring in the tent and then a loud moan.

*"Slowly now, creep along the edge."*

But I find I cannot creep. I balance my drawn sword in my hand. I need to be sure that Stekkan is unharmed.

*"You really don't."*

I can't just walk away and leave him to his fate when I can hear sounds of pain coming from under the tent.

*"You can and you must. He is a grown man and he's made his choice."*

If I'm careful, I can peek under the edge of the pavilion.

*"Please, don't."*

I stoop to my knees, dropping the stallion's reins just for a moment.

*"We need to go. Now. We have no time for this — your warning to Swordheart is too valuable. Isn't it? Isn't that what you chose over your own life?"*

But I can't leave Stekkan in trouble.

*"Not even a trouble he made for himself?"* Vargaard pleads. *"You could spend the whole of your life trying to protect that man from himself and never succeed."*

But also, if this is truly a command tent, it's possible that the Mercy Sword and the Scourge gemstone are in there. And if I could retrieve my sword or steal the heart of all of our problems, then it would be worth taking this risk.

*"You're just trying to talk yourself into this madness,"* Vargaard says. And he's right and I know it.

But I still lift the edge of the pavilion because I just can't leave Stekkan here on his own even if he was the one who made the foolish decision that put him here.

The second my eyes adjust to the dark of the richly decorated pavilion, I see him. He's been gagged with a silken scarf, his hands tied behind him with more scarves, and his legs spread apart and tied to either leg of a chair.

Sometimes eyes can speak volumes. His are speaking now and the intermingled shame and concern are almost painful to watch. They haven't taken his bird, to my surprise. She watches me from his shoulder and then very deliberately shuffles to the edge of his shoulder and relieves herself on the woven wool rug.

A truly noble companion.

I don't need to ask who has captured him. I can see the green gem on the other side of the tent, glowing its terrible glow. On either side of it, displayed like trophies, are two swords. One, I recognize as the Mercy Sword, and even though our situation is dire, my palms tingle to have it back. The other, I do not recognize, but it is close in style with very minor differences in the set of the hilt and the pattern of the designs that climb to the pommel. Is it, perhaps, another of the seven swords? Could I be so lucky?

*"It's not luck that we are here. It's stupidity. And now we must leave."*

Is he calling me stupid? But Stekkan doesn't look hurt – he only looks fearful and excited? That can't be right.

*"Scourges! Up! Get up!"*

But I'm not fast enough. My hair is yanked – hard – and my wrist wrenched so that I lose my grip on the sword. I bite back a cry, fighting against the guard holding me, but my hair is in my eyes, fallen from its tie. I can't see properly and by the time I *do* see, there are shackles around my wrists. I stumble as they shove me forward. They've attached some kind of pole to my wrists manacled behind my back.

Vargaard has been busy. There are bodies everywhere, twisted in ways no human should be. I gag, fighting my reflexes to vomit. I can't even think straight.

All I hear are curses and snapping like an angry dog. I shy from the sound only for it to follow me. and it's long moments before I realize that Vargaard is the one making that noise.

This time – for the first time – it's me trying to talk him down.

"Be the feather," I whisper. "Be the feather."

His cursing is becoming coherent.

*"A scourge on them all. I'll rip them apart."*

It looks like he already has. I'm fighting what might be hyperventilation while I try to talk him down. "Be the feather, be the feather."

The pole shoves me forward and I stumble hard to my knees.

*"I have failed you and now you are bound."* His words sound as if they have been ripped from his chest.

We are shoved unceremoniously between two furious guards.

One snaps at whoever holds me – I can't turn enough to see.

"This is what the fuss was about?"

I hear my stallion scream and I go cold. Someone is hurting him, and I cannot stop it. And Vargaard warned me not to do this.

"You laugh now, but you won't when you see what she did to Malan and Brende. And Hythin and Gorde. And Falchius."

The guard grunts, leaning out of my way as I'm shoved through the entrance of the big tent. I hear a choking sound behind me as the cloth brushes across my head, pulling my long hair into my face again.

*"They brought us near enough that I could reach the guard. The mouthy one."*

Oh.

*"He will speak no more. Of you or of anyone."*

I should be filled with revulsion, but I only feel the queasiness of worry.

The inside of the tent is lit with lanterns hung at intervals around the perimeter and from the center poles where the pavilion is highest. Their light makes the shadows dance strangely and I can't tell if that's good or bad for Vargaard's movements.

*"Bad. There is not enough light to give you much of a shadow and it's mostly overhead."*

He's stuck where I am, then, kept on a long pole.

Right in front of me, the princess leans over Stekkan. His eyes are bright, and his lips are swollen, and I wonder what they've done to him. She tenses and I expect her to hit him. I'm flinching already in anticipation of it.

I am wrong.

I feel my eyebrows lift as she leans in, settling herself between Stekkan's spread knees, takes his scruffy chin between her hands, and kisses him with masterful thoroughness.

His eyes are wide, and they meet mine for a moment over her shoulder before they snap closed.

"Mercy!" the macaw screeches.

I feel hot all over. I shouldn't be watching this.

Jendaya's hand snakes out and snatches the macaw. She flings poor Mercy to the ground without even breaking the kiss.

I gasp.

"Mercy. Oh, how the mighty fall! Mercy," the bird grumbles, creeping low across the ground to huddle against my feet. To my surprise, I'm comforted by the bird's trembling warmth as much as she seems to be by mine.

Stekkan must feel comforted, too – or something. When next I glance back his shirt is entirely unbuttoned and spread open and Jendaya's hands are splayed over his brown chest, tangled in the dark hair that forms a "T" shape over his torso as her mouth practically swallows him up.

I should look away. I really should. There are others in the room making the quiet noises of people who also think they should look away. But it's as mesmerizing as watching a man bait a bull or a snake charmer reach into the basket for a poisonous viper.

I cannot look away.

*"Merciful Divine, scrub my memories."* Vargaard's voice is dry.

"Found the girl, princess," the guard behind me says, utterly unconcerned by what he's watching. Is this, then, what has swollen Stekkan's lips? I cannot tell from the look of him if he enjoys it or hates it. But why, then, was he screaming?

Jendaya pulls up from her kiss with a gasp and a laugh, leaning her weight on straight arms rooted on the tops of Stekkan's thighs. She bites her lower lip seductively.

"I … I …" he says, his jaw dropping open torn once again between horror and enjoyment. I shake my head. There's no understanding men.

*"Some men."*

And then she kisses him one last time, grasping his black hair with one hand and tilting his head all the way back. I think she might like owning him. She might like making him do as she likes – a plaything not a man.

I find I'm angry at the thought. Complicated Stekkan – with moods that leap and jump like a fish but a sense of honor so tied up in his land that it won't bend or break or even shatter – is as human as a man can be. He's not a poppet to be played with roughly and tossed aside. It bothers me seeing him used this way.

When Jendaya's done she laughs again, steps back, and says, "You'll marry me. And you'll like it. Look at you. There's no hiding that you do."

His face is so red I could paint a sunset with it.

"I did like it," he confesses and his voice is deep with shame. "So much. And I always wanted to marry a princess. And you make me feel like a real duke – like I could reign over nations and do it well and master anything I put my hand to."

"Mmm hmm," she says absently, walking over to her green gem with a sway to her hips that isn't usually there.

"You can't marry him now," a voice says, and I realize from his uniform – a thing I've only seen illustrated in books – that this is a general from Ghregoiren. Anger slices through my fear and pain. Stekkan went to them with a warning, and this is what they did to him. The general's long legs stretch out in front of him as he takes a drink from his goblet. He's pointedly ignoring me. "He knows what you are, and he won't be used as a pawn against his people."

*"I see no key from where I am. Not on the generals nor on the princess. This is going to be a problem."*

A key. That's right. I should be trying to escape.

I am starting to think I may not leave this tent. It almost makes it worse that no one has acknowledged me here yet – they're playing this pantomime in front of me as if I am a ghost hovering, invisible, over their shoulders.

*"I will find a way to free you. I swear it on my soul."*

The princess raises an eyebrow and it's the first time she looks at me. Her smile grows as if she is taunting us both with her next words. "Won't he? I think he's just waiting to be used by the right woman."

"If you marry him, you'll have to keep him close," the Ghregoiren says again. "Under constant – and loyal – guard. You cannot trust him, or let him have any kind of freedom. Is a blood tie to Ghregoiren worth so much to you? You could marry me for the same result and have half the trouble."

The princess laughs a tinkling laugh though she's still looking at me. I am her great audience, it seems.

"You jest, I hope, General Suavenfoil. I would no more marry you than I would that bird."

He grunts.

"We are here for three more days," the princess says lightly. "And entertainment is scarce. I shall keep him and if I find no use for him by the end of those days, I shall give him to you. Can we agree on that?"

The general grunts again.

"You need to deal with the Admiral's daughter, Princess," General Ferdown says, and I turn to see him. He has a nasty bruise still healing on his face from where I last saw him in our fight at the monastery. "This is the second time she's chased after you. You know what they call Admiral Redtide – the Hound of the Seas. Never was a name so well deserved. Once he has a thing between his teeth, he never lets go. It seems his daughter is the same."

*"I just need one of them to step close enough,"* Vargaard growls. *"Just one."*

"I have my own plans for the Admiral's daughter," Jendaya says.

"I don't advise – " he begins, but she cuts him off with a gesture.

"You forget yourself, General. I will ask your advice when I need it and you will not offer it until then. For now, to remind you all that I do not want or request unsolicited counsel, I will marry Duke Catterrail and set in stone our treaty through marriage."

I catch the generals exchange a glance and then quickly look away, but by the tight expressions on their faces, I know she has them caught up so tightly that they can deny her nothing.

Jendaya kisses Stekkan again, and I see his hands flinch against his bonds as if he longs to touch her with more than his bruised lips. He can barely breathe when she's finished and none of us can bear to look at him in the eye.

When she moves back, Stekkan looks from the generals to Jendaya and back again and then his face falls even further.

"But you're evil Jendaya. And it makes me feel like I might be evil ... because I still want you."

I want to put my hand over my face. Does the duke want every woman?

*"To be fair, I think he only wanted you to keep his hide in one piece. He wants her for ... the usual reasons a man wants a woman. And he's shockingly open about it."*

That's Stekkan for you. Shockingly open.

"You're not evil," Jendaya says, looking at Stekkan for just long enough to roll her bright blue eyes. "If you were, you'd be so much better than you are right now."

The look on Stekkan's face when he looks back at her is naked longing and now, I do look away because – well because I should have looked away minutes ago and I'm only just now realizing how utterly embarrassing this is.

Vargaard seems to shudder behind me. *"Do not. Under any circumstances. Speak of this."*

He's more embarrassed than I am.

Why does Stekkan allow this?

*"Allow what? He's bound."*

But he seems complicit. He poured his heart out.

*"Remember how I told you that dukes are just as bound to place and position as anyone? He's used to living his life before servants. He doesn't worry about that as you or I might."*

"Do we have to be here for this, Princess Jendaya," one of the generals asks.

She waves a hand. "If you want to go, then leave. I'll deal with both our prisoners."

She shoots me a look to remind me that she hasn't forgotten her audience. The guard behind me clears his throat but she ignores him. He's stuck here for as long as I am. Jendaya has never been one to worry about other people's comfort.

And I wonder why she's putting on this performance at all. Why make the generals watch her toy with Stekkan? Why remind them that they are somehow under her thumb? Why do it in front of an audience? Jendaya is not trivial. She is doing this for a reason.

*"Maybe that's the reason. Humiliation. She can humiliate them for being part of this melodrama, humiliate Stekkan as her toy, and humiliate you as the leashed dog and she can do it all at once in a way that none of you can forget – or me, for that matter."*

Unfortunately, the generals slink out too far away from me as if I am a danger even manacled.

*"You are."*

"Princess?" the duke says when they are gone. "Might I beg one favor?"

"Hmm?" she asks, and she's gone back to the gem now, done with Stekkan when there's no audience to watch her play with her meat. She lifts it in one hand and something that looks like a pendant made of green glass in the other.

"Could you spare the Admiral's daughter?"

*"And just when I've lost all faith in the duke, he always surprises me,"* Vargaard says.

I agree. He's clearly obsessed with her, despite everything, and she's clearly toying with him and considering just killing him despite that. And yet he's asking for mercy for *me*?

"No," Jendaya says baldly. "But I'll tell you what. I'll let you keep her soul as a trinket. My wedding gift to you."

# Chapter Fourteen

The guard behind my back clears his throat and shakes the pole in a way that makes the manacles dig into my flesh. I flinch from the pain of it.

I've felt very little pain before these past days – before the princess let loose her scourge. I've never been thirsty or hungry and it couldn't be fixed within minutes or hours. Never been cold and not able to wrap a blanket around my shoulders. Never been tired and not able to find my bed.

I have drifted down the beach clasping my hands to my chest and thought myself a tragic figure because my father was going to marry me away to a man not of my choosing. I have missed him so much it felt like needles thrust into my chest. I have ached with missing my long-dead mother, only a shadowed memory now.

And I thought that was pain.

I am realizing now that what I thought was suffering was only an echo of all I will now taste, and I quake a little in the knowing. I am happy my hair is in my face. It keeps some of that hidden. I am not strong enough for what comes next.

*"You are."*

I am not ready.

*"None of us are ever ready."*

I am too soft. I have lived all my life in books and dreams with no thought that I would one day live in blood and steel.

*"And it is your softness I so treasure."*

And he sounds sincere. He sounds ready.

"You're awfully quiet, Ilsaletta," my rival says as she goes to an iron-bound chest decorated fancifully with mermaids interlocked by their flowing hair. It makes me think of my own hair. Are Jendaya and I interlocked in history as those poor fish-women are? Will we find the threads of fate have tangled us just as thoroughly? And what would happen if one of those mermaids tried to cut off her thick locks – would she lose all her beauty only to find herself still trapped?

Jendaya draws out a book, large and leatherbound. Thicker than two of her wrists side by side. When she opens it, I strain to look at the pages. There are diagrams – unfamiliar to me. There's a map of a place I've never seen.

I feel Vargaard flinch.

I think for a moment and then I speak. "Your home had flowers that smelled of honey and little birds that darted from bush to bush and sang sweet songs. I remember your mother had a freckle just under one eye and she held your hand and tucked your hair behind your ear as she smiled at my mother. And my mother was happy that day and everything tasted like cinnamon and smelled like the sun warming the grass."

Perhaps her home still matters enough to her to stop her hand.

"Good," Jendaya says with a smile. "The last person I tried

this with pleaded for her life and I do hate repeat performances. I appreciate your discretion."

"Your father's stables contain the finest horses – so fine that traders from all five of our neighbors come to him with cartloads of gold for just a chance at owning one from his bloodlines." Can she not remember all the reasons she shouldn't do this. "You can ride any one of them. Jump them. Race them. Feel the warmth of their muscles and the strength of their animal souls. You could do that instead, if you want a thrill."

She ignores me.

"I don't think she cares much for horses," Stekkan says quietly, and I look past Jendaya to meet his eyes. His smile is sour and twisted and his eyes wide with guilt. "She likes things a lot faster and more violent than a horse race."

"Horse races can be violent."

He snorts. "I know. I nearly lost an eye from a friend's whip the last time I raced. But you shouldn't have come, monster hunter. This is no horse race."

This time it's my turn to blush. He is correct.

*"He is correct."*

I want to sink into the earth but instead, I manage, "I thought I heard you scream."

His face is red now and my eyes have adjusted enough to notice a bruise on one cheek. "The guards did not believe I was the Duke of Catterail until the General confirmed it. They were harsh in their treatment."

Were? He's still tied up. And his chin drops in forlorn sadness.

"I've made a terrible mistake," he confesses.

"Yes, you have," Jendaya agrees coldly as if she can kiss him one moment and torture him the next.

*"Five graves. That's how we'd bury her kind."*

But there's just something about Stekkan admitting to being in trouble that makes me want to save him.

*"Let's work on saving you, first. I believe the guard behind you has the key to these manacles. I think that perhaps if you twist suddenly to the side, we can rip the pole from his hands."*

It's worth a try.

"Mmm, here it is," Jendaya murmurs, flipping a last page with triumph. She turns to where the swords are, running her hand over their hilts. Something in me jars at the sight of her touching the mercy sword. I want that back.

*"Quickly, before she makes her next move."*

He's right, of course. Quickly, I dodge to the side, twisting my arms and pivoting with my hips.

To my shock, the pole doesn't budge.

"Stay still now, prisoner," the guard says grimly, his lantern jaw clenched hard as a stone.

I struggle again and succeed only in hurting my own wrists. My eyes smart with tears at the pain in my wrists and the helplessness of being bound.

Jendaya looks up only long enough to smirk and I feel my cheeks heating. Even with all my strength, I don't have the power to move my captor.

"You've made a terrible mistake, too, Ilsaletta," Stekkan say sadly.

Jendaya lifts one of the swords – still in its scabbard – with sudden determination, running her finger over the designs inlaid in ivory on the scabbard. They are sea creatures, and her touch is a caress.

"If the generals won't stay to watch, you'll be my audience, Stekkan Falrune of House Catterrail. Do you know anything of the Spirit Principle?"

"I do not. But I beg you to spare her life," Stekkan says hopelessly and his eyes still soften when he looks at her as if he's under a spell.

*"No spell. Only the usual softening of a man toward a woman he cares for."*

He's insane.

*"No doubt."*

"I have already told you I will give you her soul," Jendaya runs the pommel down his cheek in a move both flirtatious and dominating. "Now, stop whining and watch. If I do this correctly, it will be a wonder as you've never before seen. And I think I can do it. I activated the gem in much the same way. With the power of the Nakuraki."

I feel Vargaard freeze. I don't know how I feel it. It's more of a sensation than anything else. Like her words have stolen everything from him at once.

I echo the feeling. I know my eyes are as wide as they can go, but they widen even further as she slowly, deliberately frees the sword from its scabbard.

My knees are like jelly.

*"Steady now. Steady."* Vargaard is trying to coach me, but he seems just as shaken – or is that excitement in his voice.

"I am told," Jendaya says, as she slowly, oh so slowly, draws the sword, "that the sword you had is called the Mercy Sword. It's a dark thing, curved and black and I'm given to understand your father was told not to take it from its box."

One of her eyebrows raises in a question and I've never seen a face so lovely and so utterly terrifying. I feel like I might shatter. I swallow, trying to get enough moisture in my mouth to reply but I can't.

"It's a pity you didn't break the rules to better purpose, Ilsaletta, for it seems your sword is empty though it did give to you the gifts of a monster hunter. What it didn't give you, was the true reward."

The sword slides the rest of the way from the sheath and in its shadow springs a man of shadow and dark, spirit and violence. This Nakuraki feels like what Vargaard has warned me of. He feels like evil distilled and decanted over the ages into this black stain on the land, this terrifying creature of nightmare. Oh, he's man-shaped. And he flickers as Vargaard does from one mode of dress to the next, one set of adornments to another, as if his spirit can't remember what his body ought to be. But this feels different. This is not the Nakuraki I have learned to depend on, the warrior who guards my heart, the shadow who protects my every step. This is something utterly foreign.

*"I have been warning you that I am no man."*

He is not this, either. And yet, this makes no sense. The book said only the good could be made Nakuraki.

*"What?!"*

I had not known how to tell him.

Vargaard is silenced again – this time in a way that feels different. He is not horrified. He is reverent.

"You call me from the depths, Dark Princess," the new Nakuraki says, and his voice is like bones grating against each other.

It takes me a heartbeat to realize he speaks aloud and not in my head. It's only Stekkan's face that tips me off. His mouth is gaping and his eyes dart around the room seeking where the voice comes from.

He cannot see the Nakuraki. But why can I? Jendaya doesn't see Vargaard. Why can I see her shadow warrior?

*"Yes. Why?"* Vargaard says but it feels flat, like his own mind hasn't restarted from where it was forced to stop.

"I call you up, Spirit Sword," Jendaya says in a commanding voice. "I call you up to work a wonder."

"With an audience," the Nakuraki grinds out and his eyes are wide as he stares at Vargaard and me – as if he is as worried as Vargaard is to find another of his kind. He gasps and for a moment his eyes are full of hope. "Reborn. New."

"Tell this enemy of mine who you are," Jendaya demands. She doesn't seem to realize he can see Vargaard.

"I am Haszinth the Sixth of that name, Cho'kahrin of the Blue Amazula and Lord Ruler of the Geruund people, made now Nakuraki and placed in the spirit sword."

Jendaya smiles. "And tell my enemy the difference between

your sword and this other beside me."

"The Mercy Sword takes pain and multiplies it. The Spirit soul takes the spirit and multiplies it."

"As you did when you helped me open the green gem?" Jendaya prompts.

"Wait, it had to be opened?" Stekkan says from where he is bound. "Someone had to open it and you did that? On purpose?"

We all ignore him.

"And as you will do to help me put this rival of mine into this amulet? As it says is possible in the Tomb of the Dead Kings of the Nazharai Plains."

"Will I?" the Nakuraki asks.

*"Are you not reborn with the drawing of the sword?"* Vargaard asks reverently.

The Nakuraki is looking right at him, blazing jealousy in his eyes as he replies. "There is no mercy in my sword, no kindness in its depths. I was born only once. I have not changed. I have lived each moment of deadening stillness. I have kept every memory. I have relived my life a thousand times, each mistake, each regret, each agonizing defeat."

"Mercy," the macaw whispers at my feet.

"Yes," Jendaya says impatiently, and I can tell she didn't hear Vargaard's question when she presses, holding up the green glass pendant and letting it dangle from the gold chain, "and with that glorious history, you will help me do the same to this rival of mine, trapping her soul in this bit of green glass."

"Yes," the Nakuraki agrees.

"*No!*" Vargaard screams, shoving himself between us, but he's only the barest skim of shadow and there's nothing he can do, no way he can fight. Everyone is out of reach.

I've never felt him so panicked. His emotions slice through mine like thrown daggers. He's furious and impotent and trembling.

And the other Nakuraki – Haszinth – smiles.

"I should remind you," Stekkan says and to my shock, his chin is held high with all the dignity of a duke, "that I will not wed you if you harm the Admiral's daughter. Nor will I further dally with you, Princess Jendaya. Nor will I influence my people on your behalf."

Warmth fills me – because that's the last thing he has to barter and he's trying to use it to barter for me. And on top of that, I'm pretty sure he likes dallying with Jendaya and will be sorry to stop.

No one is listening, but that doesn't make his promise empty. It makes it full of loyalty and nobility and the kind of bone-deep honor that would give away its last scrap for another. I meet his eyes and try to show my gratitude. I can do nothing for him, and he can do nothing for me, and yet somehow our mutual helplessness makes us kindred in a way I've been with no one else but Vargaard.

"Mercy. How the mighty fall," the macaw whispers at my feet.

Oh, and maybe the bird.

"This matters to you," Haszinth says, completely ignoring the duke and me. He's stretching forward, not close enough to Vargaard to be touched but just outside his reach, almost as if he can't help himself. I can tell he wants to ask question, wants to say more, but he's maintaining the illusion that Vargaard isn't there.

"Yes," Jendaya says, her eyes alight with ambition.

"*Yes,*" Vargaard says, hopelessness drawing the syllable out.

"Then I shall fill the gem with her soul." Haszinth flickers rapidly as if the excitement of the declaration is draining him and to my shock, Jendaya nicks her wrist with the Spirit Sword, letting her blood bathe the blade.

"*Ilsaletta,*" Vargaard says, shifting now so his back is to the Princess and his face is toward me. He puts his shadow hands on either side of my face. I can't ignore how they tremble like leaves. "*Look at me now and listen well. I have sworn to guard you with the last drop of my blood.*"

The other Nakuraki laughs nastily.

"*I have sworn to face down the darkness for you.*"

And now I'm starting to really understand how serious this is because he looks like he thinks he'll be coaching me through death itself.

His shadow-self swallows.

Oh.

He will be doing *exactly* that.

I can't help the tremble of my lower lip. Vargaard leans in and brushes a shadow kiss – unfelt and yet treasured – across my lips and runs his shadow hands up and down my arms as if to give me courage, but of course, I can't feel it, I can't feel him and I just want to feel someone's arms around me.

"*Isaletta, my sun and my sky. Look at me. Look.*"

I meet his eyes and there's so much broken bravery and I won't look away. I dare not look away even as they flicker and fade in and out with his jagged courage.

"It is like a death to pluck the soul from the world," Haszinth murmurs. "Beautiful, glorious death."

Jendaya whispers, enthralled. "Take my spirit with my blood and use it to unlock the world beyond."

But I don't look at her, I look only at Vargaard.

"I really don't think you should do that," Stekkan says shakily. "You are already at risk of infection from cutting yourself with an unclean blade, and now you want to unlock worlds beyond? There could be anything in there. Monsters, anything. And you're about to do something magically unkind to the only monster hunter I know despite my asking you not to and I really just think you should stop and think this through."

It takes a lot of confidence to keep talking when no one is listening.

I match my tremulous smile to Vargaard's and I refuse to let them see how terrified I am.

And then the macaw, screams exactly in Stekkan's voice, and there's a feeling like shrinking and tugging all at once, my manacles fall off, and I lose track of Vargaard as the glass pendant gets bigger and bigger until it's like a rip in the universe. With it so big, I can see through to the other side of the rip and what I see makes my heart feel like it might stop entirely.

I reach for my sword and remember it's missing.

Within the rip, hands reach for me, and bodies crawl up and over each other desperately trying to claw their way up out of the opening forming along the glass. Their howling is louder than my crashing heart, more insistent than the pull dragging me into this slash between worlds. They are wraith thin. They are tangible as gossamer lace. They are jagged splinters in the spirit world as if something has taken root where it ought not to be.

And I cannot resist as I'm gathered up and flung into their writhing mass and the world I once knew is left behind in a blink of the eye.

# NAKURAKI

I've lost her, my sun, my star. I've lost her.

Panic is rough claws tearing through me. Fear is slicing knives. I search, spinning around me so quickly that I take nothing in. I thrash out in every direction but there are only ghast-like bodies everywhere climbing over one another in their desperate bid for escape. A foot finds purchase on my elbow. Another on my knee. They're clawing over me before I can stop them, and they'll crush her like this. They'll trample my sweet Vali like the delicate petals of a full-blown rose.

Sobs claw up my throat, slashing through my vocal cords. I see a glimpse of soft brown skin through the masses, and with a roar, I lunge. I must fight with blade and fists, force each inch forward, shake my enemies off me like a dog shakes off flies, and it takes me forever to reach her and it takes me mere minutes. It's just in time and it feels too late, and I lean down and scoop her up and drape her over my neck. She's limp as a discarded dress, but she will survive this. I must believe it.

I have nothing else to believe in, anymore.

They press and heave like one massive living thing made up of a thousand dead creatures. But I press harder. I heave harder.

Soon, I am climbing on their backs and forcing my way onto their shoulders. My sword is slick with their black oily blood and my teeth are clenched against their masses and if this is hell then I am glad I am with her for I shall bear her, somehow back to heaven.

I fight for what feels like hours. Every muscle of me aches.

I fight for what feels like days. My very thoughts are lead in my brain.

Above me, the Fisher King dangles a line. He'd take my soul, drawn up from this bleak place on his line of hope. He's bleeding from his side, a slow fountain, but when he sees the burden slung over my shoulder he winks – one savior to another – and turns back to his holy work, leaving me to mine.

I fight for what feels for years until even the face of the one I am fighting for seems dim in my clouding vision.

I cannot fail her.

She has no one else to believe in, either.

# Chapter Fifteen

I do not know how long I have been immobile, unable to move my head or arms enough to see. I hear the moans of the spirits surrounding us, hear Vargaard's rough breathing, feel his muscles tense beneath my limp body as he fights for us. It's the first time I've ever felt him in the flesh – and no wonder I can, because he is all violence and certainty, lifting me up and over one horror after another. Or perhaps, I would always feel him in this place where we are both souls adrift in a sea of other souls and nothing else.

If this is what it is like on the other side, then no wonder so many souls try to break through and colonize the corricles when mortals open the door for them. I would leave this place if I could, too.

*"This is not the other side,"* I hear Vargaard faintly as if he is far away. *"This is a place in between – the Sea of Souls. You must not fear that in death you will come here. The Fisher of Souls shall catch you from here and take you to the islands of the dead beyond this place. He would not leave you in this sea."*

Then who are these in the sea? For there are many.

*"I do not know, but I feel from them a great evil, as I always do when I am forced to wait in this place."*

My heart is an egg, and the shell has cracked. He has had to wait here before?

*"Many times."*

It's a stream of thought I feel we've had before. My mind drifts often and will not settle. I do now know if I have been his burden for hours or weeks.

*"Never a burden, not to me."*

And I think he's said that to me before, too.

I long for just a drop of water, just a moment of rest.

I feel, almost like a hum, Vargaard's matching longing. And I don't know how long we are humming together. It might be moments. It might be months.

With a suddenness like being pushed off a ledge, the morass of spirits is gone, and I feel myself swelling up.

I panic, breathing hard.

A hand claps over my mouth. It is not helping. A scream starts to form in the back of my throat and then there's a scuffling sound and light flares around me.

Stekkan is in front of me, a solitary finger over his lips. He's breathing hard, one lip swollen and cut, a lantern beside him. The scuffling was him lifting the hood from the lantern. I'm slumped on a cold stone ledge in front of him and he's crouched in a squat under a sloped stone ceiling. It feels as if we are in a tomb.

He takes his hand away from my mouth and I pull myself up to sitting. My hair brushes the ceiling. My arms tremble under my weight like I have been very ill.

Vargaard.

"*I'm here.*" There's wonder in his voice.

He must be behind me, the lantern is the only thing casting a shadow though there is a crack of light. I shift, almost automatically to bring him to my side instead of at my back. Beside us is the shape of a door and beside that, a stack of baskets. They are old and thick with dust, and as my eyes adjust to the darkness, I see that Stekkan is also dust-streaked. He wears a bright orange jacket in the exact shade of the fruit my father carefully ferried home to me one year after a voyage to the north. It's highlighted with dark smudges.

My eyes stop when they fall on the green glass pendant, hanging around his neck from the fine gold chain. My prison.

Stekkan swallows. "I can't believe it worked."

"*He freed us? Him?*"

"The voice – the disembodied voice – it was talking to Jendaya and it said that only great love or great sacrifice could bring back a soul once it had been sent in the flesh into the Sea of Souls."

"You freed me," I whisper, acknowledging him. His eyebrows rise at my rough voice, and he scrambles to offer me water. He has a small flask that he shoves into my hands as if he's nervous that he hasn't been fast enough.

"He said one would make a vow and press their lips to the glass. But I wasn't sure … I didn't think. I …"

I drink long and deep and then manage, "Thank you."

"*The Spirit Sword. I should have known it would affect different things than the Mercy Sword does, but it becomes clear. Where the sword I was bound to extracts pain from the bearer, gathers it up and may unleash it at will, so this spirit sword must be able to extract spirit, store it up, and deposit it at will – in this case, into the necklace."*

That didn't explain how it also extracted my body.

*"I don't think it did."*

I'm confused but he presses.

*"Look at what you are wearing."*

I'm dressed in soft white cloth swathed around me like a burial dress.

My heart thuds painfully. Wait.

"Stekkan," I ask and I'm trying so hard to keep my voice steady. "Are we in a crypt?"

"Yes," he whispers nervously.

"Is this … my crypt?" I press.

He hangs his head. "I begged her to bury you properly – in the crypts of my family. And she agreed. My second wedding present, she said."

He looks so sad. I want to comfort him.

*"Easy now. Wait. We don't have the whole story. What vows did he say before he kissed that glass?"*

"I think you need to tell me the rest," I say to Stekkan, taking another sip of water. I am trying not to think about how long I have been thought dead or what might have happened to my body while I was not in it.

"Yes," Stekkan says, and I don't know how he manages to hang his head even farther, but he recovers after a moment, his face lighting as he reaches behind him and sets something on my lap. "But first, take this. It will help."

It's the Mercy Sword. I set my hand on its handle and almost want to sink back into the stone slab. Relief fills my aching muscles and washes over me like waves. No. Not waves. I never want to think about waves or oceans again.

"I don't know how to say this," Stekkan whispers, but I've learned that with him it's best to wait. "But I will confess, I came here hoping that maybe I could call you out, too."

Too?

"But it wasn't you who I said vows for or put my blood and kiss on the glass pendant."

It wasn't? But he doesn't know about Vargaard.

Vargaard is laughing in my head.

"I mean I would have. After. I brought the sword for you."

I'm only getting more confused.

"It was Mercy," he says, his voice cracking and a tiny traitor part of me wants to laugh with Vargaard. "Did you see her in there?"

"I did not," I say, trying to be grave against a background of Vargaard's chuckles. "But I thank you all the same."

"Obviously, I would have tried to call you out once she was safe," he says, sounding miserable.

"You don't need to confess this, Stekkan," I say, and I wonder if perhaps he isn't ten years younger than me rather than ten years older.

He looks up at me. "It gets worse."

"How much worse?" I ask, but I can't help the impatience in my voice. I'm cold. This dress is so gossamer fine I can nearly see right through it any place that the cloth isn't folded over itself. It is not enough protection against the cold of the grave – or even enough protection for my modesty. And what did they put in those baskets buried with me?

"I'm married," he says. "To Jendaya. She made me speak vows to her last night in front of a priest wreathed in white smoke and an angry smoke-ram. It's how I made my way down here. She left me in my chambers to prepare for her and …"

Vargaard chokes in the back of my head, and I hastily cut Stekkan off.

"And you escaped. And you grabbed the medallion and the sword and came down to where they entombed my body – at your request – to try to rescue Mercy and me."

He seems relieved by my summary.

"Oh! I should be checking you to be sure you aren't suffering ill effects from your soul leaving your body for three days."

I feel colder.

"Three *days?*" I manage to squeak out. "Where are we?"

His words are like brimstone thrown over me.

"Swordheart. We arrived last night."

# Chapter Sixteen

"Then it's too late," I breathe, pinching the bridge of my nose. I've failed.

*"No."*

I wanted to warn Swordheart and save her people. I wanted to be *in time* to stop this.

*"You can still warn some people. Just not this city."*

But that was the point. This city was the hub and heart of Cragspear. And it was from here that the hidden roads left the city to every nearby nation. Had Jendaya already sent riders out on them to infect our neighbors? Had she already seized her father's house and taken his life?

"Your grace," I ask carefully. "Does the king know of your marriage?"

"She was going there this evening to tell him," Stekkan says miserably. "Look, I'm so sorry. I know that I offered for your hand, and you must think me the worst of blackguards."

"What?"

*"He's afraid you will be disappointed in love,"* Vargaard's deep baritone sounds both amused and uncertain.

"You had to watch as she kissed me and … as I enjoyed it. What worse torture could there be?"

*"He has a point there."*

I ignore Vargaard. It's hard enough to keep my voice smooth.

"You shouldn't trouble yourself on my account."

"I have betrayed you and left you adrift in this world," Stekkan continues putting his face in his palm. He looks like an artist's depiction of a despairing prince.

I stand – nearly bent double – and strap the Mercy Sword around my hips. It seems the best time for it.

"You really haven't," I assure him, making my actions brisk and capable to try to remind him I'm no shrinking violet. "I did not agree to marry you, nor did I think you were promised to me."

"But you called me your betrothed." His words are muffled by his hand.

"A useful subterfuge. Shall I assume we are somewhere near your estate in Swordheart?"

"In the crypts under the small temple next door. There's a passageway underground. And I brought the box – the one they say contains another sword like the one you have there." He looks a little sick. "I hope it's not like the one Jendaya has. I don't like that voice. She left it in the room with me and it kept talking and talking about the horrible things it was going to do to me … and to Mercy."

I pause to raise an eyebrow. Sometimes Stekkan seems so foolish and then he goes and does something like this, and I wonder if the foolishness is all an act. But then again, he did marry Jendaya.

*"Against his will, I think."*

"Okay, let's make a plan," I say, trying not to think about Stekkan being forcibly married. I don't like how that makes me feel like a failure. Like I should have protected him somehow.

*"But first, let him try again to get the bird."*

What?

*"His beloved bird. It's trapped in the sea of the dead."*

And Vargaard cared about that?

*"I have dwelt in that land in the times between the drawings of the sword for many years and millennium."*

Divine sovereign. I hadn't been sure if I'd understood that correctly before. That was … heavy and deep and it made me feel like something was stuck in my chest.

*"I do not want it for the bird."*

Even though he was going to kill the bird.

*"Yes."*

Stekkan is still looking at me, hopeful and worried.

"Do you want to try to make the vow and kiss the glass again?" I ask him gently. He nods, his movement sober his mouth a long line of sadness. "What did you vow the first time?"

"That I would never leave the one who exited the pendant."

I swallow. Oh dear. I seem to be more stuck with him than ever. A very tiny trickle of fondness makes me feel warm while the practical side of me wants to vomit.

"Then, perhaps, that will work again," I say carefully.

He murmurs over the glass, rubbing it over a slash on his palm and kissing it. To my surprise, a bird pops out – but not a live one – a spirit one.

Predictably, she shrieks, "Mercy! Mercy!" with utter joy as she settles on his shoulder and then climbs over his head and onto the other shoulder.

Stekkan's smile is clouded by tears of joy. He's never looked so boyish as he does now when he reaches up to caress the spirit-macaw only for his hands to slip right through.

"Oh, Mercy," he croons, "my poor girl."

"Poor girl," trills the spirit macaw.

Vargaard puts a hand over his eyes, and I press my lips tightly together. I don't know if I want to laugh or cry, too. That forsaken bird has wormed her way into my heart, too.

*"Nothing should live in the Sea of Souls."*

But now we really did need a plan.

"Stekkan," I ask when he's done greeting his pet. "How did you know you could open the glass pendant to get us out?"

"Oh," he says, looking guilty. "Oh. Jendaya had me confined to her pavilion. She likes to umm … have me nearby. And then to a carriage. And then the pavilion again and then my estate. And she had a large chest with her with that terrible sword that talks to me, and the green gem that makes people ill, and some books – and I'd read all of them before except this one."

And now he finally pulls out the book and I've been dying to know which book it is. It's better than I could have dreamed of.

It's called "*The Grimoire of Souls and their Magic*" and I've heard of this book though I've never seen it in the flesh. It's a treasure of Cragspear, kept in the vaults of the king. Which explains, perhaps, how Jendaya got it.

"I started to read it because I was bored," Stekkan says. "I didn't expect answers. But I've always been good at studying, and I was inspired by your example in the library."

"You were?"

He looks at me a little shyly, "There are many things I admire about you, Ilsaletta, though I should not mention them now that I'm a married man."

"Against your will?" I suggest, wondering if Vargaard is correct about that.

He blushes. "Even so. It turns out this book has many answers. I've read most of it, but when I found the answer to how to fish your souls back out of the necklace, I devised my escape, and … well, here we are. It's a pity Jendaya didn't keep Mercy's body."

He tries to stroke the bird and his face falls when his hand slips through her plumage, but she settles her spirit form even closer to his face as if she understands the gesture.

"It's a hard thing to love a spirit," he says forlornly, and I try very hard not to look at Vargaard at that moment. "The book certainly explained the voice in Jendaya's sword. Did you realize something … or someone … is trapped in there? A creature called a Nakuraki?"

I nod. I'm still not looking at Vargaard.

"It gave me a turn, I can admit," he says. "That's why I left it. I can't have it scolding me and threatening me constantly, even if leaving it behind leaves Jendaya with an advantage."

I'm not sure I can tell him how stupid that is without sounding angry, so I don't address it, settling for taking a very long breath instead and saying, "And the box you brought?"

"Oh! Yes. It's just outside the door. Cover the lantern."

I cover it, plunging us in darkness, and hear the scrape of stone on stone, the slide of something being dragged, and then the scrape again.

"Light, if you please," Stekkan says, and I remove the cover from the lantern again.

"Why are we hiding?" I ask as he carefully sets the box before me. The walls of this tiny room are starting to feel too close. They're starting to feel – oppressive.

"The priests," Stekkan whispers. "I barely got past them the first time."

"They don't like visitors?" I ask. "What kind of temple is this?"

He ignores that question, but his face is pale in the lantern light. "I need you if we're going to leave here, monster hunter."

And I understand. The priests have turned to corricles. I am more impressed than ever with Stekkan. It must have taken every scrap of courage to make it to my eternal resting place to deliver my soul back into my body.

*"And to swear he'd never leave your side again. You realize that means he'll never leave my side again, too. I am not one of those who was willing to marry the duke."*

No, but he was willing to marry me off to the duke, so it seems almost ironic that now he's stuck with Stekkan, too.

I lay a hand on the smooth wood of the box that holds another of the seven swords we need to defeat Jendaya.

"How long has your family had this box, Stekkan?" I ask.

"Since the time of my great, great grandfather," the duke says, reverently.

"Perhaps you should open it," I say. And if I'm being honest, I'm nervous about it, too. I found Vargaard just like this – but Jendaya found that terrible Nakuraki in the Spirit Sword.

*"And that reminds me, sun of my existence. You kept something from me, didn't you?"*

I freeze. I had let that slip, hadn't I.

*"You believe us to be good – or to have been good before what came to pass to trap us within these blades."*

The book said only the truly good could be made Nakuraki. Despite everything he believed about himself, that meant it must be true of him, too. It is something I have never doubted.

*"And Haszinth, the Sixth of that name, Cho'kahrin of the Blue Amazula and Lord Ruler of the Geruund people? Do you believe it of him?"*

What might thousands of years consciously trapped in that place – that Sea of Souls I was trapped in with Vargaard – what would that do to a person? Would it make them evil? Or only insane? Or both?

Vargaard seemed to flinch from my words, and I paused, not sure what to do or how to make it right. I'd said something wrong, and I didn't know what it was.

*"Please, have no mind. Open the box and let us see what – or*

*who – we are dealing with."*

But I didn't want to open the box. I wanted to make things right with him.

*"Please, I beg of thee. Open the box and let us not dwell on what has been exchanged between us just now."*

I waited longer. I didn't want to leave it like this. But he refused to bend and tell me what I'd done to hurt him, and so with something like a mental sigh, I turned to Stekkan.

"There's nothing for it. Let's open your box and hope whatever is in it doesn't snatch our souls."

"Mercy," said the flickering spirit bird on his shoulder.

"Mercy," Stekkan echoed, biting his lip, and reaching for my hand.

I held it for a moment and then let it go. I had no lock picks. But I didn't need one. I reached for my sword and then stopped as Stekken smirked and offered me a small silver key.

"It's a pretty box," he said. "No need to break it, too. Enough of us are broken already."

# NAKURAKI

We are back in the world of mortals, but I am badly shaken, though I try to keep it from her. My failure to combat the power of the other Nakuraki will weigh on me now, and I will let it. Let it grind me into the ground if it means I am more vigilant. I do not burden her with the depths of my shame. She has enough to burden her. She does not need my barren apologies or hollow recriminations.

She does not need to know that seeing her in that place was so much worse than being there myself. That it nearly broke me. That it nearly left me a wisp of shadow and useless to her.

I must be strong. I must find the limits of what I've anchored myself to so that we can never again be caught off guard by my failings.

And whatever comes out of this box now, I must not trust, for I do not believe the book she read – the one that says one must be good to be made Nakuraki. I believe, instead, my own shattered glass memories of deeds that stain my hands and soul, of motivations black and twisting, and of others of my kind put into blades to serve and to find redemption.

Something tickles my mind. A memory washing through my fingers like a handful of water. Some memory of another

Nakuraki. I remember a sword. I remember a shadow. But the harder I try to seize the memory the faster it vanishes, leaving me panting with frustration.

One of the dying Vargaards lets out a sobbing keen in the back of my soul and then falls silent.

Perhaps I am mad, as she let slip. Perhaps I have lost my moorings – but if I am mad, then I am mad for her. If I have lost my mind, I have still found my sun. If I am a drifting spirit, then let me wash up upon her shores again and again.

If I can keep her alive, I will find my redemption. But I do not think Haszinth is looking for redemption and I do not trust that any other Nakuraki is still looking for it, either.

I keep close to her – closer than any natural shadow. I will be here to absorb any blow, and turn any arrow, and I will not let her know how deep the wound of my failure runs beneath my surface.

# CHAPTER SEVENTEEN

I twist the silver key into the lock and pause. Even dressed in grave clothes in my own crypt, it doesn't seem right to just open this box without a plan. But outside there are infected priests, a city that should never have seen the scourge, and the wife of my ducal friend running madly toward her kingly father.

I must do this and do it quickly.

The box opens with creaking hinges, and yes, there is a sword inside. The sword is not like the Mercy Sword that curves delicately to a point. This one is heavy and double-edged with a thickly ornate pommel, set with what looks like jade in swooping whorls and gold inlays. It's far, far too extravagant for me.

I swallow and look up at Stekkan.

"Did your family have any stories to go with this sword?"

He shakes his head. "Only warnings not to open the box."

I worry my lip between my teeth as I study it. "I think," I say after a moment, "that you should take this sword up, Stekkan."

He smirks, shaking his head. "I'm not going to hunt monsters with you, Ilsaletta Redtide. I am a duke, a healer, and now a very reluctant husband, but I am no killer."

*"You should test it first. See what manner of weapon we offer the macaw duke. Fear not, I will guard you this time. No harm will fall you from a failing of mine."*

And none ever has. He seems to shy away from the compliment. That's odd. But there's no time to dwell on that. I hear sounds beyond the door to my crypt. Soon others will be here. We need to test this sword.

I swallow down a strong stab of worry and before I can think better of it and talk myself into keeping it in the box, I grab the hilt.

What was I worrying about? It's just a sword. And to my surprise, when I lift it, it's feather-light as if I carry nothing at all. I marvel at how the light seems to catch the blade and dance down it and back again in a way that makes my eyes want to follow – and is that faint birdsong I hear in the distance? I settle back onto the stone ledge. I could sit like this forever. I see a flicker in the sword's shadow but no Nakuraki appears and if there is one, I needn't worry about it because she'd never harm me.

*"Do you hear yourself?"*

What is there to hear? I am the feather on the breeze. I start to smile as I see her appearing now in the shadow of the sword. She is fast asleep, and perhaps I should be, too. I could just lie back down on the cold stone.

*"Ilsaletta. Please put down the blade."*

Vargaard seems disturbed. But he doesn't need to be. I can set down the blade as easily as I lifted it. When I feel like it. Which isn't now.

*"Please."*

I'm smiling dreamily as I rest it back in the box and release it.

I feel like someone has struck me the moment I let go of the hilt of this sword. I suck in a long breath, gasping for air and reaching out to cling to the Mercy Sword.

*"It's okay, I have you."*

What's happening to me? My thoughts are lightning-fast and frenetic. My heart is racing. It feels like being pressed on every side as anxiety climbs up, up, up my throat. My muscles sing with tension. We need to move. We need to get going right now.

*"And you're back. If I had to guess, I would say that is the Tranquility Sword. It had an … interesting effect on your mind."*

I clear my throat. "I think you should hold onto this one, Stekkan."

"Mercy," the shadow of the macaw trills.

"Mercy," Stekkan says sadly. "But I'm not the monster hunter and I don't want to carry a sword. People who carry swords usually get attacked because people think you want to use it."

The sounds outside the crypt grow louder. Someone – or something – is drawing close.

"You don't need to use it, but someone is going to have to hold it for me," I whisper. "I'm going to have my hands full with the lantern and my own sword."

"What about the box," he whispers.

"Leave it. There's nothing in it except memories."

He nods. And I'm surprised to see he doesn't argue, just carefully jams the sword in his belt – a terrible way to carry such a priceless blade – and picks up the tome and the water flask.

"There are saddlebags outside the door," he whispers.

Now it's my turn to nod. I can't find my voice. I know we need to go out there and face this city and I don't feel ready. Not at all.

*"If you wait, then the priests will come and take you unawares. Or they might take the gear Stekkan brought, and you'll be short on supplies. We need horses again. Fast horses."*

But to ride where? I'm already picking up the lantern, the Mercy Sword held before me as if it can ward off evil – which it can, since Vargaard will direct it.

*"Ride anywhere but here. The city above will be like Seamark, only this time there is no hope of getting to the king and stopping Jendaya. If she left to find him when the duke escaped, then she's there by now. He took his time gathering what he needed. You know he's not quick. "*

I look back at Stekkan who is still adjusting the sword in his belt. He's certainly not quick. And yet, he was my salvation – and Vargaard's too.

*"I beg of you, don't remind me."*

So, we needed a new plan.

"Surely someone in this city is good – someone we can go to with our information and worries. Someone who can resist Jendaya."

"But who?" Stekkan says, finally pleased with his burden.

"The church?" I suggest.

*"No, "*Vargaard says at the same time that Stekkan says, "No."

"Remember the priest?" Stekkan hisses. "He betrayed us."

"That doesn't mean they all will."

"The ones here are no better. I'd be more comfortable looking for Istraverda House or your king's guards. There are usually a few good men among any group of guards – it's a thankless job for the truly faithful, and the Istraverdans are men of honor."

I stare at him. "And the embassy of Ghregoiren?"

His face seems almost to break in two. "No."

I want to ask more but there's a sound outside the door and then it's wrenched open and light trickles in around the shape of a tall man in vestments. He's cracked down the middle from forehead to sternum, the sides of his face and neck falling roughly to either side and the space between them is full of a boiling, bubbling yellow smoke that puffs and spurts like I'd imagine a sick dragon to do. He makes a sound – partly from his ruined, bifurcated mouth, and partly from the depths of the smoke.

Stekkan screams. His shout is so loud that my ears shoot with pain and I grimace, stepping in front of him, lamp held high, sword out.

*"Not enough space to maneuver in here. Forward!"*

I obey.

*"Rush him. Slide to his right."*

My hair is in my face, and I can't even see what we're doing, but I hear what was once a priest roaring, and then I hear his friends behind him. They're making a sound that's almost like a chant and an ululating scream all rolled into one. It shivers through my ears and directly into my skull into whatever part of me is left over from the days when men hid in caves of the jungle as animals feasted on their brothers. That part is screaming at me to run.

I do not run. I toss my head enough to see through the wave of hair - I'm going to have to tie it back or braid it – and I catch just flashes of action as I quickly obey Vargaard's barked orders.

*"Duck low. Lower."*

I gasp. I'm looking at boots stained with blood.

*"Tuck your chin and lunge upward – fast!"*

I obey and something parts against my skull but doesn't provide enough resistance to hurt. I struggle to see.

*"You don't want to see this. Quick pivot back on your left foot and hold onto that sword."*

I do as he says, strands of hair flying. The Mercy Sword connects with something, sticking and pulling, but I hold on, dragging it through.

*"Quick step backward. There you go. Lantern high and leap."*

Leap?

*"Leap! Now! Now!"*

I swallow my objections and leap, hoping he knows what he's doing.

*"When have I ever …"*

His thoughts fade off into something that feels like shame, but I can't pursue it because he's ordering me again.

*"Two paces forward and then on one knee and slide."*

To my relief, the slide blows my hair back and I can see again. I leap to my feet and twist around, jaw falling as I see Vargaard grappling with a massive husk that was once a priest. This is not the one we began the fighting against. This one is darker-skinned and his face even more ruined, as if it had been staved in with a shovel before he took in a spirit from the other side.

*"Sword up, both hands!"*

I react on instinct, bringing the sword up and bracing my spread feet. Vargaard slams the husk onto my sword and the action drives me to my knees. Pain shudders up the bone and my eyes smart for a moment but when they clear the area is still.

I carefully extract the husk from the end of the Mercy Sword, keeping it in my grip as it bears the edge of the pain I feel from fighting. Who would have thought winning would hurt this much.

*"It always does."*

There are … far more bodies than I expected. Five. No. Six, I think. It's hard to tell. There are more pieces than I'd like and a smell that … uh oh.

I vomit. And then have to do it a second time.

As soon as I'm done, I scurry backward until my back hits a pillar, trying not to heave a third time.

*"Easy now, book girl. Easy now, Vali. My sun, my stars. You are safe."*

Safe and extremely nauseated – and not just by how many … parts … I'm seeing but by the smell filling what looks like a long-arched hall carved into the earth and buttressed with white stone. There are little doors along it – crypts, of course – with inscriptions on some and even little icons set into niches to honor the dead there. Brackets are set for torches, but the only light anywhere is the one bobbing in my trembling hand.

"Mercy," Stekkan breathes like a curse, or maybe a prayer.

I hold the lantern higher so I can see him there, standing in the door of what must have been my crypt, saddlebags slung over either shoulder, the tome clutched to his chest, the spirit bird stunned into silence on one shoulder. His forehead is marked by a spray of blood.

"There's blood on your forehead," I say helpfully.

"There's blood on your ... everything," he says, swallowing, and I look down on what had once been a gauzy white dress and realize to my horror that he is right.

We're silent for a moment and in that moment, a footfall sounds. My blade is up before I realize it, my heart hammering, my shadow guardian alert and spread out as far as he can ahead of me, one hand clawed out and the other gripping his sword as if he will shred with his hand what he misses with his blade. Maybe he will. I was blessedly blind for most of that last encounter.

"Hello?" a quavering voice says.

"State your name!" I demand, and I hate that I sound like a really young woman and I hate even more that I sound scared and shaken.

"I'm Felicitous Quarning, of the City Watch?" he says like it's a question. "Umm, is someone alive in all that ... that viscera?"

# CHAPTER EIGHTEEN

I step out toward the voice. "We're here."

The young man blanches at the sight of me dripping with blood. "Umm, your pardon miss, but the Duchess of Severna requests that all living people within the church join her above."

"Severna?" Stekkan asks, stumbling forward with the book pressed against his chest. His eyes are bright. Is that hope I see? It stands in stark contrast to the horror in the young city watchman's eyes. Stekkan hastily grabs the edge of a small tapestry decorating the door to a crypt and wipes his face clean – or cleaner. The blood smears more than disappears.

He shouldn't desecrate the dwellings of the dead.

*"They won't mind. They are past that now."*

But I do.

*"You've already desecrated quite a lot."*

"Sir," the guard says, saluting promptly. He's trying very hard not to look down the hall at us, but his face is green and drawn and I can tell he's about to try to upstage my vomit performance.

"But how did she …" Stekkan shakes his head, puzzled, and then he's pressing forward – to my utter shock – and hurrying up the wide marble stairs leaving thick crimson smears in his wake.

The city watchman gapes after him. I'm tempted to close his mouth for him, but the mutterings of the spirit bird – "*Mercy, mercy, mercy,*" are growing fainter and I don't trust the city to be kind to Stekkan. Even now that he's Prince of Cragspear. That's still settling in on me. I should be addressing him that way. He can't inherit. Inheritance here is all in the bloodlines, but he's owed as much respect as the princess.

I hurry to follow, but I keep my blade drawn. I don't know what's above. The boy looks uninjured as he hurries to follow me – and I don't know why my mind keeps calling him that when he's the same age as me.

"*It's because he's fresh. He's not seen much death, this one.*"

Neither had I, a fortnight ago.

"Miss, lady," he asks breathlessly, following in my wake. "Are there priests down here? Only, I was sent to find priests."

"We're the only priests you're going to find," I say, sadly, and I'm surprised to find there's a lump in my throat. We share this – the boy and I. We both thought there would be goodness in this church – something that remained past this desecration. And we're both violently wrong.

The marble stairs are wide and shallow – perfect for people carrying the dead down to the crypts under the church. As we reach the top, it opens into a wide, beautiful, round room set in marble. There are graceful statues at five points around the room, a domed ceiling, and concentric benches around a center mosaic. I'd stop and admire it if I wasn't trying to chase Stekkan down – and if there weren't two priests slumped over the benches. That made two who had died instantly, and six-ish who had turned evil, and so far, zero running to our aid or calling us to theirs.

Not one righteous priest. The thought feels like a knife wound.

*"Organized religions often draw those who want to organize others into patterns of their own choosing. I'd say that's true for whatever Order this is."*

"Umm, miss?" Felicitous Quarning queries. "What are you priests of, if I can ask?"

"Shadows and sorrows," I say sharply. I should be kinder, but I find the smell of death in the air is sapping my patience. And so are the tears just behind my surface.

*"Don't cry for those who would never cry for you. Think, instead, how we can cut a swath through more of their kind."*

I need to be stronger. I need to be faster.

*"I am already all that for you. All you need to be is brave."*

"Which of you is the shadow and which is the sorrow?" the watchman asks as if he's studying to take exams.

*"I'll be the shadow,"* Vargaard says grimly, which works well for me, since I have the sorrow part well covered.

Stekkan still hasn't turned, and now he's out the door, light flaring and then dimming as it opens and closes.

"Divine Sovereign help us!" I curse.

I've never seen him run like this even when we've been chased by monsters. What does he know about this Severna and why is he running to meet her and leaving me behind where I can't keep him safe?

Vargaard is cursing with me, and so is the guard, so at least we all agree on one thing.

I pick up my pace, determined to find the duke – prince? – before he's ripped apart by monsters. I can hear their ululating cries far in the distance as I breach the high, peaked door. Even from so far away, they chill my blood like the first tendrils of winter reaching across the ground to breathe death over frost-vulnerable vegetation. They're out there. They want me. They want us all.

I'm breathless by the time I burst through the doors and look down on those gathered around the church steps. They hold torches in one hand and swords in the other. Some of them are mounted – though not all, I notice. There are city watch in dull grey jackets with round helmets like Quarning's and palace guard with their little feather tufts in their hats and blue jackets, and random men in fine silk coats with swords more meant for decoration than use brandished in their kid-gloved hands, and some men with tall peaked hats dressed in a style I've only seen in books. It's the military guard of Cantimar and behind them, astride a stallion fit for cavalry, is a woman in a fitted coat that flares across her hips.

"Stekkan! My poor boy!" she is saying, arms flung wide as she reaches for him. I'm stunned enough to freeze. How many women does Stekkan have stashed around the country? Sweethearts of every nation, I'd think since this one is dressed like she's Cantimarian and looks old enough to be his mother.

"Aunt Dahlia," he says, relief lacing his words.

That explains it. Those high nobles of every country are so intermarried that they're all cousins, or nephews, or aunts.

They're embracing and making the sounds of family reunited and I take that moment to look over her gathered companions.

There are no civilians other than the men with the pretty

silk coats who are doubtlessly lordlings. All the rest are guard or watch or military. And there are no women except "Aunt Dahlia," which seems odd to me.

Her people look lost, but I see people coming from the surrounding buildings – more churches mostly and a few elaborate manor houses. Each of them looks as ill as Quarning does. He edges to the side to whisper to an older man in watchman grey. The man looks lost, too, as if he still doesn't believe what he's seeing. There's blood on the edge of his weapon.

*"And on the blades of the soldiers – Cantimarians, you called them. None on the blades of the lordlings."*

No surprises there. I'd judge them for it, but I'm no more capable than they are without Vargaard guiding me. They're terrified and trying not to show it, but their horses' eyes roll and their feet dance sideways, betraying their riders' terror.

*"As anyone would be in the middle of a scourge. I'd say this woman is likely a diplomat here at court. She must be a smart one to have gathered up this force and be on her way out of the city. Perhaps she will make it to her home nation in time to warn them."*

Or to spread it to them.

*"If she's very smart she'll prevent that."*

This feels like a repeat of Seamark, except this woman isn't sheltering orphaned children. I want to know why. How can she truly be good and yet not be worried about the innocents caught up in this?

*"Good has many battles to fight. Not every tool of righteousness is the right one for every battle that needs to be fought. The duke is a good man, and yet I'd never ask him to fight with his sword in defense of this city."*

"This is not the place for you, my dear nephew," Aunt Dahlia, the Duchess of Severna, is saying. "We need fighters, not lovers. Tell me you aren't in trouble again."

"I might be in a little trouble, Aunt," Stekkan says with one of his dimpled grins. "But in my defense, I have brought with me the greatest monster hunter of Cragspear."

She snorts. "We could use him. These things descended on the embassy an hour ago, killing everything in sight. My entire household is gone except what you see here – and some died not by the blade but in the most peculiar of ways. I've had to make do with conscripts from the guards here," she points lazily at the watchman and palace guard she has with her. "We're about to fight our way to the palace. The king will have to let us in to help with the defenses. And then when we have a better idea what is going on here, we may decide to return to Cantimar."

It's too late for the king. But will she believe me when I tell her that?

"Then why are you here?" Stekkan said, looking around the square.

"You, primarily." His aunt is brisk. "If there was any chance you'd resurfaced from whatever dalliance you disappeared to during the ball, I could hardly abandon you. But also, I'm looking for priests. We're dealing with some kind of outbreak of the demonic. I shudder to tell you the things I have seen."

"I think I have some idea," Stekkan says.

She gives him a long look. "I believe you do, dear boy. So, here we came looking for holy men, and of course, that's the one time you can't find one of those little terriers nipping at your heels. It's like they know they're needed and now they've made themselves scarce."

"I'm afraid they're dead, Aunt Dahlia," Stekkan says in a way that seems to be trying to comfort her while breaking the news.

"All of them?" she asks in horror.

"All the ones in the church where I was found in," Stekkan says.

"And the others?" she looks to the older guard who was whispering with Quarning. He clears his throat before giving his report.

"Our scouts are back. The buildings are empty of the living. There were many dead. One church showed signs of a struggle but held no corpses, just items broken and tossed about as if someone was packing quickly. One was … filled?" He looks at Quarning who nods sickly. "With carnage."

I feel myself frowning. That doesn't make sense to me.

*"Most people, you must remember are neither terribly good nor noticeably evil. They simply die from the scourge. These houses of priests must have been among them."*

And the temple that showed signs of leaving? Would that be the good fleeing or the evil on the hunt?

*"It's too hard to say for sure. Keep your eyes watching. Perhaps we'll learn."*

"There are no women with you," Stekkan says, finally looking around him.

"Of course not, nephew. I sent those of them who survived out with the rest of those I'd recruited. They'll head to our diplomatic house in Heraultway. Hopefully, that house has not been attacked, too."

She looks worried. "Why is this demon force attacking diplomats and temples?"

"It's not a demon force," Stekkan says as the howls in the background begin again. "It's a sickness. It spreads from person to person."

At his words everyone seems to draw back, looking at those around them. The Duchess of Severna swallows.

"How do you know?" she asks in a low voice.

"This is the third place, I've seen," Stekkan says, and then suddenly she has a dagger out and against his chest and he throws his hands up, fingers wide in surrender. "Please, Aunt Dahlia!"

"Don't 'Aunt Dahlia' me when you're the one spreading this vileness from town to town."

*"If you want to keep your little pet, I'd suggest interfering right around now."*

Oh. Yes. I'd been so caught up in the drama I hadn't remembered that I should speak.

I clear my throat.

Everyone looks at me.

"The Prince of Cragspear hasn't spread this disease," I say calmly and I'm careful to keep my shoulders back and my chin high, so no one sees how nervous I am to be addressing them all.

*"That's right. Look confident and they will take you seriously. Offer them strength and in strength, they will respond."*

"I'm not talking to a prince," the Duchess of Severna says, biting off each word. "I'm speaking to my nephew the Duke of Catterail. If he told you he's a prince, well, he's lied to pretty girls before and I'm sure he'll lie again."

"You're mistaken," I say coolly. "And doubly so if you plan to go to the palace. The scourge has gone there before you and by now the king is likely dead, eight in ten of his advisors, court, servants, and family will be dead with him. Another one in ten of them will have joined the demonic evil you have witnessed and chosen to fight. And the rest we must leave to the mercy of the Divine Sovereign because we are far too late to save them."

"And how would you know, you lace-garbed, fresh-faced maiden?"

Stekkan clears his throat quietly.

"Yes, nephew?" She doesn't turn her gaze from mine.

"Um. That's the monster hunter I told you about."

And now everyone is silent, and I feel my cheeks flame hot. And I want to deny it. But if I do, they won't listen to my warning. I lick my lips and part them and I don't know what I'm going to say. How do you sway a crowd of adults when they look more lost than you? How do you speak to royals when you're nothing more than a hopped-up ship captain's daughter?

I don't have to respond. The howl starts again and this time, it's right on top of us. The first guard falls with a cut-off scream and I barely have time to draw my blade before they're everywhere.

# Chapter Nineteen

*"Follow in my footsteps,"* Vargaard barks. *"Go! Go!"*

I'm moving before I realize it, feet falling in the prints of his shadow. He's barely ahead of me, but he whirls so that his shadow stays in front, his back to the lights carried by the main group.

I stumble over my skirts and pause to tear the filmy, semi-transparent linen as close as I can to the knee. It's indecent. And it might save my life.

*"I will save your life, not the tearing of skirts."*

But I run easier this way. And the dress will need to be replaced anyway.

*"Ready, now. Two hands on your weapon and brace your footing."*

I'm quick to obey, bracing myself between two men on stallions as the monsters that once were human break upon us like a wave.

From the view of the Duchess in her saddle, this is probably a sight to behold — and she can probably see the larger action — who is charging, who retreating, where our enemies pour in from and where we ought to go to hold them off. I see none of that. In this, as in all that has preceded it since my birthday night, I am too close to see the movements and patterns, too deeply in the battle to be able to note the tides and turns that drive it. The history reader within me is frustrated by it. The girl in me is just grateful to be alive.

Vargaard grunts in my mind as the first monster slams into his shadow form, but he's already dodging and leaping, evading the strike of the first once-human creature while darting around to stab it in the back.

The creature falls onto my blade. I know how this goes now. It shouldn't be so hard to brace myself for the impact and take it as it rips at the muscles of my arms through the sword. Even so, I'm trembling as I brace a foot on the shoulder of the man who looks like he might have been a baker – is that flour on his shirt and trousers? – and with trembling arms and heaving breaths, I yank my sword from his flesh.

I should be used to it. But I am not. I may never be.

*"Follow me, now."* Vargaard's low growl is firm but calm, like the sound of the sea waves lapping against the shore – so constant in a world where nothing else is. And I hold onto it as he dances me through the movements.

To the side, a twist, my blade out, retrieve it, and try not to look – oh Divine Sovereign, please say that's not what I think it is coming from his skull – and now we dance again and I wish I could close my eyes and let Vargaard be my eyes for me, let him lead where I dare barely to follow. But he cannot. I must see this myself. I must listen to their screams.

*"I cannot save you from what I must do to them, but I can save you from what they would do to you."*

I cling to his voice, and I am the feather, floating as we weave and work.

From very far away, I hear Stekkan saying, "I told you she was a monster hunter."

"I see," the Duchess says, and she sounds deeply shaken.

"Has she done this before?" someone asks in a well-bred tone but the wonder in his voice cannot be masked.

"She rescued me from manacles and fought our way free," Stekkan says fervently, "and then she fought a path clear through this scourge in Seamark."

There is a grunt beside me, and the next part is elaborate, taking all my concentration to keep up with Vargaard. I can hear nothing but my own huffed breath between the cries of friends and foes. I am so deeply into our work that I barely twist my blade away when one of the Cantimarians almost skewers himself on it. I spin at the last second and Vargaard plants his spirit sword into the man's attacker. The Cantimarian's eyes are wide, and his jaw drops open as he watches me.

I feel my cheeks growing hot. I am doing nothing but following Vargaard. Any help being offered is his help. It's his skill that guides my feet and blade. His penetrating mind that always seems to determine the exact right place to put us to turn one attack after another. He's not flawless – he's already sustained a blow that leaves his left shadow leg dragging as he moves – but he's still quick and unhesitating.

We turn again, catching a husk in the back and ripping the flesh from his ribs along his back, exposing his spine. My gut knots painfully at the sight and the sound of his scream, but the knot of City Watchmen we've saved look up with such desperate relief that all I can do is look back with parted lips and an aching heart when I see two of them clutching a comrade who will certainly never stand again. His legs are missing and blood flows over his lower lip.

Tears come to my eyes. He's someone's child. He's someone's friend. And just like that, his life is taken. And why?

*"Because a princess and her ambitions let hell loose over us all."*

Yes.

*"Because all men have a vein of darkness running through them. And some of them are not content to leave it buried far below, but dig it up with the fervor of a merchant finding silver."*

All men? But what about those too good to be turned by the scourge?

*"Even them."*

How can he be sure? I wonder as we spin to look up at a man far too large to be human.

*"I have waded through the Sea of Souls. I have seen the Fisher King. I have drunk the cup of death. I know."*

But I'm not listening. I'm trying to control my bladder and the shaking in my hands as the giant lumbers toward us. He wears a palace guard uniform and has a cockade on his hat.

I hear a whisper building behind me, and I realize the screams have died. I wrench my terrified gaze away from the giant for just a moment. He is our last standing adversary right now, and behind me – far behind me – three full horse lengths – a group of guards on foot have sword and shield raised to form a wall among the heaps of dead. Behind them are those on horse.

Mercy breaks free from Stekkan's shoulder, screaming in her ghostly voice, *"Mercy! Mercy! Mercy!"*

I shiver and turn but not before I catch the looks of marveling wonder shared on every face – looks almost of worship. Who had this man been that still, they look at him this way?

*"It's not him they're looking at,"* Vargaard tells me.

Then who?

"I told you she was marvelous," Stekkan whispers so loudly it could carry across the entire square. And at the sounds of assent behind me, I want to sink into the ground. It isn't me. It's all Vargaard.

*"I live in your shadow, my sun, my center. And it is my greatest honor that every eye look to you in the same manner that I do."*

I'm gutted by the responsibility of it. I feel ill. But I don't have time to feel ill for long.

The giant is done looking at me and assessing. Now, he strikes.

*"Focus. Sword tip up."*

I do as I'm ordered at the same time that Vargaard barely dodges the first blow from within the shadow.

*"Dive! Dive!"*

I barely manage to comply, diving to the cobblestones under the sweep of the husk's arm. Stone scrapes my forearms and chest as I slide across the rough stones.

*"On your feet."*

And I'm back up again, barely knowing how I got there. I suck in a deep breath at the same moment that Vargaard strikes, once, twice, three times, and then is struck in turn. The hit is square in his chest, and he flies as far as his shadow can go without disconnecting with me and then seems to almost snap as it comes back to my feet again. He wavers for a moment and in the pause of his attack, the giant roars, his voice reverberating from the buildings around and then before my eyes – to my utter horror – his face cracks with a sound like wood being split, and smoke pours out the smoke between eyes, along the bridge of a nose, and from a ruined nose, rising in a roiling puff of red to double his height and swirl around him, renewing his strength.

He lifts his chest, leans his head back, and roars. And I'm stunned. Too stunned to move.

*"Move! Roll! Get to his ankle."*

I roll, biting down on my own tongue as I fight the fear and horror bubbling inside me, fighting my desperate attempt to hold onto the feather. As I roll, I catch little glimpses of those watching us. They're limned in moonlight and torchlight, bathed as if half-gilded and then set in place to dry, with mouths hanging open to catch the memory and eyes as wide as a fish hauled from the depths into the poison of the air. Wonder and horror, worship and dismay – they are all this and more. And so am I from my place even closer to the action.

I feel Vargaard's grim determination as he struggles behind me. I feel him buckle.

*"Don't turn. Use the Mercy Sword to slice his hamstring. That's right. Over the ankle."*

He has thick leather boots.

*"Jam the sword into the ankle and bear all your weight against it and we'll hope you hit flesh and not bone."*

I grit my teeth, hearing his battle above me, and somehow – how? – feeling as he twists and aches and bears up under blows that would shatter a man of flesh. And I know they are agonizing because I feel the agony in him, skittering like butter over a very hot pan as I line up my sword with the man's ankle and then seat the pommel against my shoulder and thrust it forward with every bit of my might.

The Mercy Sword glimmers in the darkness and unleashes its own dark fury as it slices through leather and flesh and tendon. I grit my teeth, pray the Fisher King will take me to the other side someday, and rip the Mercy Sword against the back of his boot.

He screams in an awful, muffled way as if the scream won't come out.

"*Roll, roll, roll!*" Vargaard's voice is faint.

But I'm already rolling, and as I roll, I feel my enemy fall beside me.

"*Your knife!*"

I drop the sword to reach for the knife. Pain bowls me over, blackening my thoughts and leaving my own cry stuck in my throat. I hadn't even realized I was injured. But every bit of me screams with agony.

I can still move. Blindly I fumble for my knife and get it out in time to see his head hit the cobbles beside me, eyes open and parted around roiling red smoke.

"*The heart.*"

I need no more guidance. I reach over and plunge the knife into his heart with every bit of energy I have left.

And then we are both lying on the cobbles, eye to terrible eye, heaving – but he is heaving his last breath through his cloven chest and I'm heaving out my relief and horror, my guilt and grim duty. And I think I'm choking on a sob because I can't do this anymore. I am not death's handmaiden. I'm just a girl. I'm just a girl.

And then the sight of him is gone, disguised in the darkness as a shadow slides violently between us – so violently that I can see Vargaard's perfect face in all its exact detail as he forces himself between us and all his demanding passion as he swoops toward me and I want him to carry me away as he did in the Sea of Souls. And I want to hide in his shadow forever. And I want to be his alone and gone from this world of horror. And for just a moment I feel his violent kiss before it trembles into tenderness and is gone like the last scrap of smoke from a blown candle.

I sigh. For though I want him with all my trembling soul, he will never be mine – not to hold and not truly to have for when I die, he will go on.

*"My Ilsaletta."* His deep voice has a burr of pain in it. *"I have been meaning to tell you – I am mortal with you now. When you die, I will die with you. When you grow old. You will only grow into my agedness and together, one day, we will pass through the Sea of Souls to the other side. Fear not, tangled roots of my heart, for even were you to forsake me, I shall never forsake you. Even were you to turn your face from me, still, I shall wait in your shadow to bear you across that tide. Though you take another for lover – and you really should – and feel the comfort of his flesh-and-blood warmth, still I will wait for you as the mountains wait for their return to the sea and the skies await the fires of heaven to burn them up, so I will wait for you. Heart of my heart, life of my life, you will never be any more alone now than you want to be."*

I'm sobbing now. Shaking like a fool or a hurt child and I don't know how to dislodge this tangle in my chest of fear and exhaustion and … I think maybe love. But I can't seem to stop. It's like I've broken, and I can't put the pieces back together.

I hear him groan and then suddenly he's gone. More injured

than I thought. More pained. He's gone to bleed in the silence of my shadow. And his loss only makes me sob harder – and not in a pretty way – in the way where your nose and mouth are running with your eyes into a swollen puddle.

And just when I think I'll never be okay again, there are arms around me. Real arms.

"It's okay, monster hunter," Stekkan whispers. "I've got you."

"Does this happen a lot?" an imperious voice asks from above me.

"Mercy," the macaw hisses censoriously. She's found Stekkan's shoulder again.

"Of course, it does," Stekkan growls, and to my surprise, I realize he's crouched over me defensively. "Don't you realize that this kind of magic takes its toll?"

# Chapter Twenty

I don't need my Nakuraki here to tell me that I need to pull myself together. It takes all my willpower, but I manage to pull my sobs into a huffing, gasping breathing instead and then, with all the strength of will I have, to suck in one long inhale and stop altogether. I'm still trembling after, and my tears flow silently, but I've stopped sobbing.

The Duchess gives me one sharp nod of approval.

"If you don't mind, Aunt, I have some extra clothes for the monster hunter," Stekkan says calmly, not looking at my face and I realize why. He's no fool our duke – prince. And he's keeping up this aura of respect to shield me. If I don't help him quickly, it will crumble as fast as it was built.

I force myself to my feet, chin high, ignoring how little is left of the flimsy dress I'd been buried in. I think most of the bodice has torn off with the skirt, but so much of me is swathed in blood, that I still feel clothed – or at least coated.

I try not to think of myself as a half-naked girl, but as a warrior. No warrior need be ashamed of victory. My tears stop and with a final sniff, I put them behind me. I am ready for the next battle.

"Give us a moment's leave to ready for the next battle," Stekkan says respectfully, but he doesn't wait for her nod. He hustles me over to the fountain in the middle of the square, making it look like he's merely escorting me, though his grip on my arm is so strong that it's like a vice and his pace so fast that I can barely keep up.

"Monster hunter," he says when we get there, and to my shock he bows. As he's still lowered, he whispers hastily. "We must maintain this pretense or lose what little we've gained. Wash. Quickly. I'll cover for you."

I don't smile gratefully. That would ruin the ruse.

"Thank you, my prince," I say precisely and step under the fountain, not caring that it's freezing cold or that it soaks me through, only glad for the water washing away the gore sticking to my skin.   The water sluices it away and renews my resolve. I am the feather. I am untouched by the blood washing over me. I am untouched by the cold.

I look into the eyes of anyone who looks at me. But most of them look away quickly with heated cheeks or satisfied looks. They see nothing but bravery and victory when they look at me. And I think some of them even see hope. Their eyes are shining.

I step out from the water, clear-eyed, and to my surprise, Stekkan is offering me a pair of close breeches, and a frilly white shirt, and a bright fuchsia jacket.  His – I believe.

*"Oh, how the mighty fall!"* Mercy shrieks as I hurriedly don them, but I don't feel fallen. Or mighty. I feel like forged metal. Back from the refiner's fire. Back from the beating and shaping. Not eager. Not happy. But ready.

"I kept something else for you," Stekkan says cautiously, but when I turn it's my father's coat. I can barely breathe for a moment. Gratitude, it seems, is a breathless thing. I put it on hurriedly.

Stekkan hands me my scabbard, clean from the waterfall, and the Mercy Sword and as I buckle it on and sheathe the sword, I keep my hand on the pommel to heal my aches and pains – I've definitely pulled my ribs and there are pains in all my healing injuries – and then I hold my head up and speak.

"Lead on, Prince Stekkan."

His eyes are tight, and a muscle is bouncing in his jaw, but he's as aware of the eyes as I am, and he turns briskly and marches back toward his aunt.

"I'll require a mount," he said, mouth grim. "And then we need to leave this place. The city is lost, and with it, all of Cragspear. Our only hope now is to warn the rest."

"You're truly married, then?" she says looking troubled. "To Princess Jendaya."

His nod is tight.

"You cannot inherit."

"Nor do I mean to. Do you see anything here I would want to inherit?" He gestures around us at the dead monsters that used to be people, at the glow in the sky beyond where I'm pretty sure there's a fire being lit – Again. What is it with Jendaya and fires? – and at the few men staring at him.

His aunt barks a laugh as a dead man's mount is offered to Stekkan. "Agreed. Lead on then, my prince."

He mounts it with a more confident attitude than I've seen from him before. I'm certain it is a show and worried about what is underneath it. Is he also gibbering in fear under the smooth face he offers his audience? Is he also trying to think through what feels like mud clogging in his brain? I'm not certain, but when he reaches down to offer me the pillion seat behind him, I take it without hesitation. If there is one person living in this world right now who understands how precarious our hope is like I do, it's Stekkan.

"I think I should hold onto the book," he tells me, and I know it's to keep my sword arm free, though he makes it sound like a declaration of some kind. He's very, very good at pretending to be royal.

Guilt stabs through me as I realize it's not pretending. And I wonder, as we begin to ride, picking our way carefully between bodies and rubble, what Jendaya forced on him with that marriage, what might have happened in those three days that I lay dead, and he was truly alone in this world. He fingers the gem around his neck absently and I think that perhaps his eyes have lines around them that weren't there before.

And is it so terrible that I'm happy to have a friend with me? Is it so terrible to be glad I'm not alone? Perhaps it is, knowing how he came to be here.

We pick our way slowly through the debris, the guard fanning out before us and behind us. The city is a maze of dead ends where parts of houses or shops have rained down to fill the streets and ways blocked off by the sounds of screaming and running feet that tell us bands of husks and corricles are ravaging the city there.

Each turn scrapes at the nerves. The man who rides beside us jumps at every turn and with each new encounter, I feel more anxious for my Nakuraki? How long will he need to heal? Should I call him back now? Should I wait for longer?

I'll wait, I tell myself. I'll wait until I can't wait anymore.

But I'm realizing that just as the Mercy Sword siphons my pain, so my shadow siphons my worries. Just as it gives me deep, quick healing, so he gives me peace. And I miss him badly as we creep through the city.

It's hours later when Stekkan whispers to me. Even his whisper feels too loud. We've done nothing but whisper this whole time. An hour ago, we tied flour sacks found at a bakery around the horses' hooves to mask the sounds of our journey.

"Each blocked road drives us closer to the palace and Swordheart square," he whispers, and I feel a chill go through me. He surreptitiously takes one of my hands and I don't know if that's for him or for me, but we're united in one thing – neither of us wants to be anywhere near his new bride.

"Have you heard the story of Asandrata?" I whisper in his ear.

"I have not," he whispers back.

"She was queen of Marana about a thousand years ago," I whisper.

"Did she own one of these swords?" he whispers back.

His aunt gives us a reproving look. But he needs this. And I will give him what he needs right now just like he sheltered me when I needed it.

"She married a man thirty years younger than her," I whisper to him. "And a month after their wedding they both drank wine – a present from their ally across the Coruvan channel – and the queen died immediately. The wine was poisoned by her ally, for all her allies and all her people hated her for the atrocities she made them bear."

"And the prince?" Stekkan asks, his voice shaking, and he looks at me and I realize I've grown so used to those brown eyes it would gut me to see him hurt. I can smell his scent of roses and sandalwood and I think he deserves better than life as Jendaya's body slave in all but name.

"He lived," I whisper. "The stories say he was spared for his pure heart and innocence – spared by the Divine Sovereign for he could no more help his captivity to her than could any of her subjects."

Stekkan releases my hand, nodding soberly, and to my surprise, he takes out the glass pendant from around his neck, closes his eyes and kisses it. "May it be so and may it ever be so."

We ride quietly around another turn, then backtrack from yet another mound of rubble until we find another path to try. Ahead, a watchman whistles the signal for hostiles and Stekkan turns and catches my eye. His eyes are steel as he whispers to me in a voice shaking with vulnerability.

"Monster hunter?"

"My prince?"

"Will you hunt a monster for me?"

And we both know what he means and what my reply is when I seize his hand and hold it firmly with all my resolve. He pulls it up to his lips and kisses it – but it's not a kiss of affection. It's the kiss a sovereign gives to his subject to seal an oath. And we are sealed now in this – a vow taken together. A vow to kill a queen.

"*Mercy,*" his spirit bird whispers.

But I find there is no mercy in my heart, nor in Stekkan's matching gaze.

# NAKURAKI

My mind is wild as I wait to be restored in her shadow. I cannot sleep or rest, even though all my senses are dulled and muffled and darkened. I feel a tingling, like little tugs coming in every direction – too many sensations to settle. It takes a long time to remember to breathe and calm myself. I must be calm for her. I am useless when I am unspooling.

With calm, comes awareness. With awareness, I can sense what I have been avoiding – that I'm losing all sense of those other Vargaards who came before me. Their dying moans are fading. The stink of their rot is no longer ever-present. I still find some memories when I reach for them, but most are nothing but mist and those I find are disconnected. I cannot remember whether the faces I see are former friends, former enemies, or even the Valis I swore to protect.

I sting with loss and yet I do not even know what I mourn.

It feels like unraveling, but when I prod at it, it's not. It's merely that I'm moored to a new foundation, made mortal in the shadow of a mortal. Custom made to fit her where once I was fit for eternity.

I am a prisoner of now.

I am still being knit back together as my awareness moves out from that, and now I sense more – I can feel the Spirit Sword somewhere in this city – feel the power it has to banish me and my beloved and it leaves me both chilled and determined. If ever I see it again, I must destroy it without hesitation. But how could that be accomplished? I lack knowledge. Would melting it in a forge be enough? Shattering it as a regular sword might be shattered? Whatever the way, I will have to take it. I dare not leave standing so powerful a threat to her.

And what if it were to separate us? What if it were to cleave us apart?

Then that is a risk I must take, for her safety ascends higher than my enjoyment of it. Her victory takes precedence over my delight in it.

I have my goal, then. And I must hold it close to my heart where none might see and snatch it away.

I float and I wait as I am stitched back together, made whole to serve her again and I burn with warm purpose at the joy of it.

# Chapter Twenty-One

We're huddled around the Duchess in a dingy alley and her face is drawn tight and lined – more so as the hours have dragged on.

"Every time we try to edge toward the city wall, we're pushed back or blocked," her guard captain says in a whisper. I've learned his name is Echobar. His handlebar mustache makes him easy to pick out. "We've been at this for hours and we've succeeded only in moving in a crescent toward the palace."

"We're being herded," Sergeant Malcolm grumbles. He's the highest-ranking of the city watchmen we have with us, and I like him because he insists on keeping watch for survivors. We've seen none yet, though we've played this game of cat and mouse across half the city. We *have* seen people scurry away before we can catch up. And we've seen buildings destroyed by gangs of husks and corricles.

"There should be more innocents," Stekkan says worriedly, voicing my thoughts.

"My pardon, your lordship," the Sergeant says, not meeting anyone's eyes, "but this is a city. People are concentrated here. It only takes a small number – as we've seen here – to destroy the rest and put the innocent to the sword. We've been watching for survivors. We've been doing all we can to find them. Instead, all we've found are things I want to wash from my eyes."

"I'm sorry," Stekkan says and this time the guard looks up and gives him a harsh nod.

Sergeant Malcolm's dirty and grizzled, but the look in his eyes when he looks at Stekkan gives me pause. I frown and look at my friend again. He looks the part of a prince right now with his eyes wide and liquid with compassion but his back ramrod straight. No one else can see the spirit bird spoiling the effect by waving her splayed tail feathers at this makeshift council.

"So, we aren't getting out by usual means. And sending birds with messages will not help get out the word of what is happening here. We could split up?"

Echobar is already shaking his head. "Begging your pardon, my lady, but there's no advantage to that. We'll just be slaughtered like chickens, one by one. They must be herding us toward the palace for a reason. The one consistent thing is that any opening toward the walls is quickly cut off."

He's right. I've seen more of this city than ever before but, lost as I feel in the labyrinth of streets, even I can tell we're being pressed toward the center."

"Perhaps there are sewers we could escape the city through?" the Duchess says hopefully, but Sergeant Malcolm is already shaking his head.

"A clever idea, my lady, but no. We have sewers, but there are grates between districts and only the watch houses, the Captain of Sewers, and the Guild of Street Cleaners have keys – and even then, only the Captain of Sewers has the keys to the whole network. The rest only have the keys to our own districts. I've been down there, and I've seen them and the gates are solid as can be. We'd not get far. A temporary hiding place, perhaps, but not an escape."

The Duchess sighs and I want to sigh with her.

"Then we go to the palace."

We all look at the officer from the palace guard. I don't know his name yet, because this is the first time, he's spoken at all. He's been blank-faced this entire time as if trying to pretend he is not in the city seeing what he is seeing. I understand. I want to wash my eyes, just like the Sergeant.

"Explain," the Duchess says wearily.

"If we're being herded, and this is the only choice left to us, then we should go strong and ready to fight, rather than ragged from pushing back against the inevitable," he says, shrugging one shoulder. "Besides, our king may still live and while he draws breath, our lives are his to spend."

To spend. I never want to think like that. To my surprise, I see a reflection of my thoughts in Stekkan's expression. But why am I surprised? The duke – prince – has already proven he has depths under his carefully crafted exterior. I should be past surprise by now.

The sounds of the streets close to this one are growing louder. There's more of that terrible chanting ululation that chills us to the core – and more screams, of course.

We're packed in the alley like fish salted and barrelled. Shoulder to shoulder, horses nose to flank. Sweat and fear mix in the air, twisting already ragged stomachs and binding tight nerves. We're all sure that death is around any turn. We know we've already spent all our luck.

"So. No birds. No sewers. No more trying to reach the walls," the Duchess says with a sigh. "I need to see. It's too limited on the ground."

On instinct, we all look up to the only thing rising above the buildings surrounding us – the cathedral spire.

"Someone could climb up," the sergeant says doubtfully. He doesn't look at his few remaining men. I don't want to, either. Most of them have been wounded over the past few hours – those who haven't died. He keeps sending them whenever he hears a cry for help, and I don't blame him for it. The city is their home. These are their people. But they've saved no one and lost half their number. And I – I can barely look him in the eye. I'm the monster hunter. I should be accompanying them in the search no matter what Stekkan has said on the matter about saving me "for later."

I know I have to wait for my Nakuraki to heal, but I can't bear their hopeful glances whenever they look at me.

"Whoever goes up might have a fight inside the cathedral first, and they'd still have to climb," Echobar says.

The nobles are silent. They spoke up in the early hours, but I've watched their spirits drain like a pond in summer. They sit slumped in their saddles, looking in every direction with troubled eyes and tight faces. They've grown to realize they can add nothing to this escape attempt. Which, I suppose, shows that the Duchess did not choose fools.

"And once they are up in the bell tower, anyone could see them. They'd be a target for the … monsters." We are all calling the husks that, though Echobar still hesitates to do that.

"If someone goes, they can raise the black flag," one of the nobles says. But he says it quietly and he won't look at the Duchess. "I'm not volunteering. I know. I'm a coward and I admit it, but I can't take heights and I wouldn't survive on my own if attacked. I'm man enough to know that."

"What is the black flag?" the Duchess asks, carefully.

No one wants to answer. Like the noble who spoke, I think they are afraid that if they answer, they'll be called upon to go.

"It means plague in the city," I volunteer. I read about this in a book about Swordheart. "Anyone who sees it would know. But you'd have to be practically within the walls to see the tower with the flag and anyone that close already knows that madness has taken this place."

There's a cough. It's the same gold-jacketed noble who made the suggestion. "There's the watcher."

"Watcher?" the Duchess asks, the steel in her voice commanding a response.

We're getting too loud. The noise one street over is growing as if enemies amass in direct response to our voices. The nobles flinch at her loud question and I almost flinch with them. The answer from gold-jacket is made in a harsh whisper as if he can force her to whisper by whispering himself.

"There's a watcher on a nearby hill in the Farseer Abbey. By routine, they look through a glass to the city three times a day after prayers. They check for the flag. It's one of their duties in exchange for support from the crown. And if they see a flag – any signal flag – then they put up their own flag to match and the Quesarian Abbey in the north and Applegate Abbey to the west will look through their glasses – "

The Duchess interrupts. "And how far does the network extend? To the borders?"

He nods.

"And it's not common knowledge?"

"If you live in the Abbeys or work for the exchequer or oversee the Guild of Messengers, you would know but," he spread his hands as if to indicate that most of those who would know are dead or soon to be.

My mouth feels dry and when I catch the despair in his eyes, I know it's reflected in mine. How many other things like this are being lost as those who know them perish?

"Then getting that flag up is our best chance to warn the nations," the Duchess says grimly. "And that means it's the most important thing we could be doing."

I agree with that.

"So, we'll send the monster hunter to sneak up and do that while the rest of us provide a distraction."

I do not agree with *that*.

"I'm not good with heights," I say carefully.

"No one else here can fend off monsters alone," the Duchess says firmly.

I look around, trying to find a gaze that will meet mine. None of them will – except Stekkan who grimaces dramatically. I thought that when I found adults, they would handle things. I mean, I'm an adult, but barely. I thought grown men and women would … well, take charge like the Duchess and do the work and I could just sort of back them up. I didn't think I'd be searching a crowd of good men – and they had to be good, or they'd be dead – looking for a single one to acknowledge that they were going to send an eighteen-year-old girl off on her own to climb a spire and hang a flag.

"You can hang the flag from the bell tower. You don't have to climb the actual spire," the Duchess says firmly.

"And you can wait in the cathedral below and back me up," I say with growing firmness. She, at least, meets my eye and I try to put all my steel into my own gaze to match hers.

She shakes her head. "You've seen how these creatures are attracted to large groups. You're more likely to succeed on your own. We will provide the distraction."

Stekkan coughs. "I don't leave the monster hunter."

"Be serious, my boy. You're no warrior. And now you're a prince. You can't be left to dangle where you'll likely die."

I like the Duchess's practical outlook. I'd like it more if it agreed with mine.

"I don't leave the monster hunter," Stekkan says again.

His aunt leans in close. "You're a man grown, Stekkan, and I won't decide for you – though I could. I could truss you up and carry you through this city and back to your mother. But I won't. Just know that if you go with her and leave this last group of loyal souls, the chances are that we two will never speak again."

"Mercy!" his bird scolds and he half-reaches for her before he seems to remember he'd look a fool petting a creature no one could see.

He clears his throat. I know he's saddened by her words. I know it like I know my own skittering emotions. He doesn't want to say goodbye to her, but he made a vow when he kissed that pendant, and my life likely depends on him keeping it.

I would never hold him to the vows – even knowing that. But I also wouldn't humiliate him by saying that before others – like he's not man enough to know his own mind and honor. I might have thought that when I first met him. I don't think it now. Too much has passed between us – too much heaviness and sorrow.

I purse my lips as I realize I also don't *want* him to go, even if it doesn't mean trapping me in the Sea of Souls again. I've grown used to Stekkan. I'm not sure what I'd do without that bird of his cursing at me.

But I stay silent, and I look away – refusing to sway him from what choice he'll make. Vargaard would say I was going soft.

*"Are you hurt?"*

I nearly gasp at his voice in my mind and then the feeling – the silky almost-there feeling of him swirling around me, never touching, but so, so close he could be wrapped up in my own soul. For a moment I don't even realize that the others are trotting away. I can barely catch my breath. He's back. He's back.

My hands stop trembling and I didn't realize they even were doing that until they stop.

Is *he* still hurt? That's the real question.

*"I have some residual injuries to bear. I'll need time to rest again – but I can fight. Where is the threat?"*

The others are already riding away, not even looking back. Stekkan sits our horse with a straight back and high head, looking toward the cathedral. Somehow, we'll fight our way in and hang the black flag from the bell tower.

*"I like clear goals. Thank you for waking me in time."*

"Are you ready, monster hunter?" Stekkan asks, and his voice doesn't waver. He looks every inch the prince he now is.

"Lead on, Stekkan, Prince of Cragspear," I say, and I draw the Mercy Sword and hold it beside us as he kicks the horse into a trot.

We move together as we ride, a ball of determination and worry with Vargaard streaming behind us in the rising dawn. We're already alone. But we've been alone this whole time and we don't need anyone else.

# CHAPTER TWENTY-TWO

The streets are quiet on the way to the cathedral – the only sound that of the distant bellowing and the sound of quiet hooves and jingling from those who left us. The silence should be welcome, but I find it worrying.

*"I don't see signs of stealth in the alleys or doorways. How long have I rested?"*

Five or six hours, perhaps. And I have missed him for every one of them.

I don't know how I can tell that he is pleased, but I can. I need to talk to him in my mind. There has been no time since I woke from the dead.

*"Then speak now, as we ride."*

How do you tell someone that you aren't sure they should wade through hell for you?

*"Don't tell me that. Tell me something else."*

How do you tell them that you owe them a debt you can never pay?

*"You owe me nothing, Vali. All that I am is yours down to my most cherished hopes and the torn dreams I still clutch to my breast."*

I bite my lip. How do I tell him that his kiss gave me life and kept me out of the darkness?

*"You tell me just like that, for it is to that purpose my embrace was offered. Your affirmation makes it whole."*

How do I tell him that I never want his kisses to end? That I want his shadows to cover my shame and his almost-touch to graze me at every turn?

My cheeks are hot. I shouldn't admit to that.

*"I will hold your confessions next to my heart, closer than any desire of my own."*

There's something stuck in my throat. I cough but it won't go away. It's making me tear up.

"Vargaard," I whisper, and I feel Stekkan shift curiously so I speak the rest in my mind. I want to tell him. I pause. I can't quite even think what I want to say but I'm afraid that if I don't tell him now, he'll never know.

*"You don't need to tell me anything, Vali. I know you like I know my own thoughts. I feel the pulse and sway of your heart. I have held your soul next to mine as I waded through the Sea of Souls and when we two find ourselves there again, I will aid you in the crossing. To the last moment the light reigns over the earth, I am yours. To your last breath. To your last thought."*

That's what I want to say. That I'm his, too.

And it feels too small a thing to give.

*"Your regard is everything. Never doubt it."*

And he does seem to swell with joy, enough that my nervous thoughts solidify to tell him my heart.

I don't ever want you to leave me.

*"Done."*

My thoughts stumble clumsily over one another but I can't stop now – I won't.

I want to love you forever, I think to him.

*"Love?"* The word shivers and thrills in his thick baritone, making it somehow deeper and fuller than my hesitant confession.

It peals like a bell between us and then heat floods around me like hot honey and I sway for a moment in warmth and closing darkness before I remember to breathe and the world around shivers back into focus.

*"Every current of my being draws to you as the tide to the moon. I ascend and recede by the beating of your heart. I am fixed in place by the steel of your existence."*

Yes, I think, and now my cheeks really will burst into flame. That. I feel like that.

He's quiet for a moment. Long enough to make me feel aware of how much of myself I've laid bare. Foolishly. For one day my father will return and want to know who he can give my heart to. One day, the world will return to what it was and there will be expectations on me, and I feel like I've made a promise with my words and stamped a seal into my heart.

*"I will never hold you to anything."*

I grit my teeth. For he has done to me what I would not do to Stekkan.

Grant me more honor than that, Vargaard, I think. Hear my

words and hold me to them, for I will hold my own honor in the same esteem I hold those words.

He's hesitating but I can feel the exaltation behind his hesitance. The deep desire to claim the vow I offer, as I have taken the one he offered me. It hovers between us, and I think he will speak and seal things in one way or another when suddenly the horse whinnies, and I'm dragged roughly back to where we are.

The wide stairs of the cathedral spread before us and at the top of the stairs stands a lone priest. He looks up when we approach, and tiny white smoke birds dance around his innocent-looking face.

"Come to confess?" he asks in a voice sweet as a child's.

*"On your left!"* Vargaard warns and then we're slammed to the side and the horse is falling with an equine scream.

# CHAPTER TWENTY-THREE

The breath rushes out of me and for one horrible moment I'm paralyzed and pinned. I try to shout but my voice has been snatched.

Sweaty horseback and the smell of Stekkan – sandalwood and masculinity – fill my nose. My face is pressed against the fine silk of his coat. I feel like I'm going to drown in it, and I can't get a breath. Can't.

And then, to my relief, the horse shifts, and I twist enough to wrench free of the pin and scramble out from under the horse's bulk. My right leg doesn't feel right. It buckles under me as I try to stand, but I hold the Mercy Sword tightly and it takes the edge of pain into its blade.

Vargaard skitters past me as I'm bringing up the blade. My shadow is very long in the spreading dawn light, and he has room to move. He's taking full advantage. He spins down the length of the shadow, flipping up into a leaping summersault at the end of it and as he completes the aerial roll, his shadow blade sticks into the priest's neck.

The priest bubbles for a moment and then collapses, but not before I see what was lurking behind him. They leap forward. One is what knocked our horse from his feet. I turn in a circle, counting.

One.

*"Mercy!"* Stekkan's spirit bird shoots past me, planting her talons on the creature's face and shrieking as she tries to rip out spirit eyes.

Two.

I catch a glimpse of Stekkan's face as I turn. He's on his feet again, hands trembling so quickly you could shake a rug with them. His mouth hangs open.

Three.

They are taller than I am. They glow with the same glow as Mercy – spirits then. The spirits of the world's largest panthers. And they each have three snarling heads – each head making its own individual rumbling growl. I do not like panthers with one head. I like them little more with three.

"Divine Sovereign," Stekkan whispers as I get my blade up. Vargaard is battling the one at my back, but he can't be three places at once. My heart is a drum beating the march of dread. "Divine Sovereign, in your kindness, look to me with mercy. Bear me swiftly over the river of death and hold my soul safe from evil. Divine Sovereign, in your kindness, look to me with mercy …"

I tune out the rote prayer and think of the Fisher King drawing souls up to his boat. I shake the image from my head and lunge toward the nearest three-headed cat.

Vargaard snaps in front of me like a slingshot loosed, his blade slashing and cutting. The cat dances to the side and then lunges around Vargaard, long arm curling toward me in a wide swipe and one head screaming his cat-scream while another hisses at me. Pride fills me as I manage to hit the blow aside with my sword. I'm getting better. But I'm still not good enough.

There's a scream behind me, high and agonized. Stekkan crumples, hand clutching his shoulder where the coat is ripped and blood pours from his shoulder. The glass pendant swings from his neck wildly as Mercy attacks the cat's face, shrieking and flapping.

I leap to stand over him – practically on top of him – blade up and feet planted and Vargaard is drawn after me. I hear him cursing but the second cat is already lunging, and I barely get my sword moving in time to slice his chest as he tries to claw my face off. His heads thrash wildly, and I wonder if they are more impairment than benefit. He screams in fury at my slash and retreats a pace.

I look back to see Vargaard has slain the third cat. He vaults over me, sliding close as my skin where I barely have a shadow, and materializing in front of me in time to catch and turn the answering strike of the last cat.

She hisses her fury with all three heads and then launches herself at him.

He times his slash perfectly, cutting her – throat to pelvis – in a single, terrible slash. I'm glad spirit cats don't have insides to spill over the ground. Glad for many reasons, but mostly because she was upon me when he sliced her. Her claw catches my cheek as she falls and pain slices sharply through me, muffled by the Mercy Sword but still throbbing and tight.

We're left with the bodies of the three-headed cats fading around us, the distant scream of our horse echoing in our ears – he's long gone now – and the sound of our own breathing in our ears. We lost the saddlebags. And our food and water stores.

Spirit panthers? With three heads? I prod at Vargaard to be

sure I'm not dreaming up this horror.

*"Yes."*

That was unexpected.

*"Indeed."*

But what does it mean?

*"It means the barriers are weakening. The monsters are not just human anymore."*

I swallow. I want to ask him to tell me more. And I also don't.

Beneath me, Stekkan groans. It's a better thing to think about, so I turn and drop into a crouch to look after him.

To my surprise, he still has the book clutched to his chest and the sword jammed in the sheath at his belt. We haven't lost the truly important things.

I set down the Mercy Sword so I can look at his shoulder and nearly moan. My leg *hurts*.

*"I don't think it's broken. I watched your movements, and it can support your weight if it must. Your ankle moves properly without dangling as it might with a sprain."*

Is he a doctor now, too?

*"I'm merely reassuring you that the pain is not a sign of something worse, merely a thing you must endure for now."*

Which is very kind of him, and I shouldn't be so snappy. It just took me by surprise and surprise pain makes a girl less generous of spirit.

*"You are doing well. Think no more of it."*

He shouldn't be so forgiving. We both know I don't deserve it.

Stekkan's coat and shirt are already shredded across his shoulder, I tear the fabric back to reveal the rest. The cuts are deep – three of them in the thick, rippling muscle of his shoulder. He looks up at me helplessly with glassy eyes.

"We have no supplies to stitch it," he says through gritted teeth.

"Maybe in the church?" I look helplessly toward the dark door – and to do that I have to look past the slain priest. I shiver.

"Bandage it tightly and that will have to do for now," he says, direct in his orders.

Doctor Stekkan is always certain and careful. I try to honor him with the same treatment, following his directions to cut a swath from the hem of my over-long shirt and bind to his wound tightly with it.

*"And now we move. We can't stay here. We're like a ringing bell to our enemies."*

He's like a wreath, surrounding me, flowing, flowing as he orbits, sharp attention bringing him more to life than ever, as if his very concentration is violent.

"Can you stand?" I ask Stekkan.

"Yes." He licks his lips, but his face is set determinedly as I help him to his feet. He holds on to the book. That makes me feel properly solid. Someone understands how important that book is. The world can be orderly again someday with people like that in it.

Even if there are only a few.

"We need to get inside," I say.

He nods and Mercy finds her seat on his good shoulder again, biting at his ear between consoling him with gentle reminders of, "Mercy. Mercy. See how the mighty fall. Mercy."

Stekkan reaches up and cups her spirit form with his palm. "I was never mighty, Mercy. But your point is well taken."

He looks as tired as I feel.

"Just one more thing," I tell him, trying to infuse my voice with confidence I don't feel. "Then we can rest."

He looks around us. "The only rest now is the rest of the dead."

I shiver, remembering the Sea of Souls. I would not have called it restful.

*"Easy now, my sun. That is not the rest of the dead. That is the sifting place. Were the Fisher King to pull you from there you would find sweet rest on the other side where honey flows in the rivers and every fruit is ripe."*

I like that. It makes me want to cry. But there is no room for tears in what comes next. Instead, I pretend I can feel the spirit hand that tangles itself for a bare moment in my hair. I close my eyes to take it in. And then I open them to what must come next.

"Stay behind me, Stekkan. There may be more of those aberrant creatures. And if there are, there's no one I'd rather have at my back than you."

He seems heartened by that. Or if not heartened, then at least resigned. He shifts the book and takes his place behind me.

*"And here I thought you preferred me at your back,"* Vargaard

says lightly. He is already ahead, scouting the length of my shadow.

"You," I say aloud. "I prefer in my heart."

"If you're talking to Mercy," Stekkan says thickly – and that must be pain thickening his voice. "Then you should know, her heart has already been claimed by me."

"Noted."

*"Noted."*

# Chapter Twenty-Four

The cathedral doors are already open when we mount the last stair.

I have never seen a cathedral before. I pause momentarily. I don't mean to, but what else is there to do when such glory spreads out before you?

Someone built this place out of marble. Well, not just someone. I've seen sketches and read the history. It was built over four generations. A tribute to the sea, I know – the source of Cragspear's wealth and glory. I have read of the workers crushed under the great stones as they were laid – how they kept laying them anyway. I have seen the plans recorded precisely and firmly with artist's copies of the cornices and moldings. Of mermaids enshrined forever in clusters under each large wave of stained glass. The glass set to look like the swell of the sea that rolls all the way up the wall to lick at the arched ceiling.

The gold of dawn strikes the blue and turquoise and clear panes and floods across the long white benches and white tiled floor and the beauty of it flays my heart open and imprints itself onto my eyes so that I can't take a breath. I almost don't want to.

*"This."*

Is it not beautiful?

*"Is what I see when I look at you."*

And now I really can't breathe.

Stekkan's half-muffled cry pulls me back to reality and I see what he's pointing mutely toward.

Five more priests glide down the long aisle of the cathedral toward us, each with white doves swirling around him and white smoke wreathing that.

I hope there are no more three-headed panthers.

But there are no other corpses anywhere – not dead ones or slain ones. Where did the other priests go?

*"I told you not to trust priests."*

But that's not enough for me.

"Where are the others?" I ask boldly.

"Shhh," Stekkan whispers behind me. "Don't talk to them!"

"The others?" the center priest asks innocently, hands tucked into the opposite sleeves and face as smooth and unlined as a child's.

"The other priests?" I ask, shifting my grip on the Mercy Sword.

They're getting closer, their feet whisper-soft on the tile.

Stekkan makes a whimpering sound.

There is not another sound in the cathedral and – somehow – it seems to block any sound from without. Did I not know what the smoke wreathing these five meant, I would think this a pool of tranquility.

"They're in the cellar," the priest in front of me says, and his round face slowly blossoms into a guileless smile. "Kept until we find use for them."

"Alive?" I ask, and my voice squeaks a little. I need to tame that tell.

"Why would they be alive?" he asks.

And then the birds all strike at once, darting toward us. I lash out with the sword.

"*Watch it!*"

But though I nearly hit Vargaard, I *do* hit the birds, shattering them to puffs of smoke.

Not fast enough. One of the priests is upon me. It's just dumb luck that gets my sword in place fast enough for him to skewer himself upon it.

"*Don't expect your other enemies to be as obliging.*"

But he's already killed another and in minutes of huffing, aching slowness, we cut them apart until the white of the long, echoing chamber meant for the sea is stained with a red tide.

I'm puffing and panting when we're done. There's a stitch in my side and I pulled something in one of my shoulders and I'm still having trouble with that leg.

I find Stekkan watching me. But he's not trembling or stammering like he used to. He just looks worn out, like he might collapse soon. I'm more worried about that than I am about screaming.

"*As you should. Tiredness and depression are surer killers than fear. But that is a wound we must bind later, if we all survive that long."*

And with that reminder, I go in search of the bell tower and the black banner.

I find both with little trouble. The stairs to the high bell tower are located off the narthex. And at the base of the tower, a large shelf carved with fanciful crabs and lobsters is stacked with banners of many colors. The black one is on the bottom of the stack, a narrow strip of it faded almost to light grey by the sun from sitting here folded for years in the stained-glass sun.

"Will you wait here?" I ask Stekkan and his laugh sounds more panicked than anything.

"I said I would stick to your back, and I meant it."

I nod. I realize I'm delaying on purpose.

*"We should ascend immediately. We know that we've killed those who would seek us harm down below. We should clear the tower of enemies before more assemble here."*

Good advice, and yet that was part of the problem. I was afraid to go up and be attacked again.

*"I will defend you."*

But he couldn't defend me from falling. It's not like he could catch me.

*"The duke will defend you."*

I almost laugh at the idea of Vargaard entrusting me to Stekkan.

*"We must use the tools we have,"* he says wryly.

But it's enough to get me moving. I heft the sword and start to climb, my aching leg screaming with every stair we climb. There are a lot of them.

The tower is square and the steps circle on the inside of the wall, ending in landings when they run out of horizontal space and then jogging to the left so that we turn left six times before we reach the top. It's so much farther than I thought it would be and even the carefully made railing that runs along the open side of the stairs is not much comfort to me. All I can think of is stories of crumbling steps falling to pieces after the hero has reached the top.

*"If that happens, I will show you how to climb down without them. I have done that before – twice. Once the stairs really did crumble and once someone set them ablaze."*

I shiver. Perhaps I should be grateful there is no fire.

*"It makes everything much more urgent."*

We reach the trapdoor at the top of the last set of stairs. It's open, but I don't want to put my head through it.

*"With the light as it is, I cannot go before you."*

My heart is in my throat.

I know I've hesitated too long when Stekkan whispers, "I could go first?"

I shake my head. Bad idea. He's the one with the crown now – though he doesn't want it and is probably more afraid of his bride than of having his head lopped off when he sticks it through that trap door.

"Why is it so quiet?" I whisper back.

"Maybe because everyone is dead?"

"But the city sounds quiet, too."

"Maybe they're all dead," he says, and I realize we're both leaning forward, shoulder to injured shoulder trying to look up through the trapdoor without putting our heads at hacking level.

With a sigh, I give up. We can't stand here forever.

I step up and through as fast as I can, as if I can outrun whatever blow awaits me.

Nothing happens. I simply find myself out of breath at the top of the stairs in a wide, open room, ringed in built-in benches. The walls are waist-high stone but otherwise open to the sky except for a pillar in each corner that together hold up a tall, peaked roof that guards a massive brass bell from the elements.

The bell hangs innocently, a frayed rope as thick as my wrist dangling from it to the clean tower floor. This tower is swept regularly. The bell rope is smooth with wear. The built-in benches worn from many priestly behinds.

And there are no monsters here except for us.

I almost sob with relief.

Until I realize I was right about the city.

It's silent.

From up here, we should hear everything down below. Instead, I don't even hear bird song.

"*I don't like this,*" Vargaard says warily.

"I don't like this," Stekkan breathes.

That's what I've been trying to say.

*"It worries me that he and I think so much alike."*

It doesn't worry me. Men of honor are often in agreement.

But I take a long breath and a very slow step forward. And then another.

I'm almost to the edge when I realize that this tower is just barely taller than the towers of the palace, which is right beside this cathedral. I didn't realize how close we were when we split from the Duchess or when we found the steps to the cathedral, but I'm realizing now that we came in a back entrance. The main entrance shares space with the palace overlooking a massive, sunken square with seven streets leading into it.

It is not empty.

But all within the packed square have their heads hung low as if bowing to a bier in their midst. There's someone on it, sleeping perhaps, or sick.

There are so many people packed into that square – more than I can count. And they spread out in every direction filling all the streets except a few in a narrow, sheltered crescent. And my heart is in my throat as I recognize that crescent. It's the way the Duchess' party had been shepherded through the city. And a city I thought was almost empty, is packed to the gills with people. I can't pick out individual faces beyond the square below, but even I can read the language of uniforms. It's the armies Jendaya has been raising that surround this square. And they roil with colored smoke.

I'm going to be sick.

No. I'm going to die. Maybe not right now, but certainly within the next hours.

*"Not as long as you cast a shadow,"* Vargaard says it like a vow.

And as if his thought is the spark lighting a blaze, a voice rings out, "And now that we have had our moment of silence, we leave the soul of my father to the gods."

My heart freezes at Jendaya's voice. I shoot a glance to my right to see Stekkan leaning over the railing, green-faced as he spots his wife.

It's her father on the bier, I realize and he's dead.

"He looks like he could be sleeping," I whisper.

"He was too nice to be good," Stekkan says sorrowfully.

"What does that mean?"

"He was always such a very nice king," Stekkan says. "I don't think he even raised his voice to the princess. But look, he died like most do – untouched. The scourge took him."

He's right. And that means he's also right that the king isn't really *good* because the good don't die that way.

"*The duke is right on many levels. Those who are very nice are rarely good. True righteousness sometimes requires the ruffling of feathers.*"

And again, they are thinking alike. I'm starting to feel like there's an echo in my head.

"*Ha! Even a broken compass is right sometimes.*"

Jendaya speaks again, and I'm astonished by how well her voice carries across the square and up to the tower.

"And look who has joined us for our crowning!" she says, graciously. "The aunt of my newly acquired husband. Is he with you, Duchess?"

Stekkan grabs my hand so hard it pinches, but I raise my other hand to stop Vargaard from pushing him aside. Because we agree on needing to hold someone right now.

Below me, the Duchess is shoved forward by a pair of men. One of them is the palace guard whose name I never learned. The one who so badly wanted to return to the palace.

It turns out, his plan is a good one after all.

Or at least it is for Jendaya.

*"Mercy,"* the macaw whispers. And it's just about the cruelest thing anyone could say because there's no mercy here at all.

# Chapter Twenty-Five

"Aunt Dahlia," Stekkan whispers.

On instinct, I reach for his hand, tucking the black flag under my arm. We both know that meeting Princess Jendaya is a death sentence for anyone who isn't wreathed in spirit smoke. That would have been us if we hadn't been sent to the cathedral. That could still be us.

The muscle in his jaw flexes as he clenches it. Whatever comes next isn't going to be something he will want to see.

"Help me with this flag," I whisper, but he doesn't listen. He's leaning on the rail as if he could leap from it and swoop down to rescue her.

It aches to watch him in a way that dwarfs the pain in my leg. Mercy paces back and forth across his hunched shoulders, agitated with his worry.

But even if I can't distract him, I still need to hang this flag and I need to do it quickly. I realize that I don't know which side of the tower to hang it on.

*"There's a metal hanger that can be hoisted just under the bell. You'd see the flag then, from any direction."*

Good idea. I hurry toward the hanger and lower it, trying not to let it squeak. Will Jendaya be able to hear us as well as we can hear her? Every movement seems to echo in my mind, making my heart stutter and speed.

*"Easy now. That sunken square is made to reverberate for public displays. The sound bounces off the walls of the palace and this cathedral and the other surrounding buildings. You won't be heard here if you don't shout, but you'll hear every word below."*

I'm fixing the first corner of the banner onto a flag hook when I hear Jendaya again.

"What shall we do with Duchess Severn, my lord duke?" Jendaya says.

"Who is she talking to?" I whisper across to Stekkan. He doesn't turn, and I can tell that he can't. He's frozen there by strong emotion.

"The Duke Jherain. Cantimar is ruled by a council made up of the rulers of the five duchies." I know this, but I don't interrupt. I'm busy looking for the other loop in this huge flag. "He's holding a sword in a scabbard in front of him, like it's ceremonial."

Oh no.

*"Scourges,"* Vargaard curses.

Stekkan's whisper grows grimmer and – I realize, with surprise – more furious as he adds, "As is Count Landsdown of Triverge. As is the Hexiplurius of Hexaluun. As is Calla Magnana of Istraverda. We both know they do not have Ghregoiren's Sword, but General Suavenfoil holds a sword all the same. Do you know what this means?"

I hook the second corner of the flag and spread the cloth out so it won't tangle, hurrying to where the pulley will raise it.

"No," I say through my teeth.

"These are all minor nobles in each country. They're her conspiracy. She's been planning this. It wasn't spurred by the moment like she claimed, just because she saw the glowing gem and was tempted."

"I think you'll find she lies a lot," I say.

"Yes." He sounds sad.

"Let her watch what she fled," I hear a voice demand from below. It's faint, but even so, I can hear the haughtiness of it.

Stekkan turns, looking back to the verdict on his aunt.

"Wait," he whispers.

"The sooner I get the flag up, the sooner we can get out of here," I whisper.

"And you don't think they won't notice from below?" he hisses back, turning finally to glare at me as he presses his point. "The moment you get the flag up they'll leave the square to come after us and we will lose this chance to catalog our adversaries. Already, we have names and faces of those who have betrayed us – and we know they have those swords."

I pause – not just because his logic has swayed me, but because of the swords. What does it mean that they have all the other seven swords?

*"I think we are about to find out. I agree with the Duke. The moment the flag rises we will have to battle our way out. Let's find out why."*

I try to look in his eyes but all I see is shadow. He leans in close so that it feels almost as if he kisses the top of my head, but my imagination is wild and I'm likely just dreaming of what I wish to be.

I nod, reluctantly and slip over to Stekkan. He doesn't look at me, but he seems calmer now that I've agreed.

"Then before those gathered here today," Jendaya's voice rings clear and true. "I declare to you the death of my father, King Mattreus Vindicus of Cragspear, and I take upon myself his crown to rule as Queen of Cragspear and Mistress of the armies of the Scourge."

The crown she is putting on her own head glitters in the sun.

"Does that make me king, then?" Stekkan asks with a bitter twist to his lips.

"*Oh, how the mighty fall!*" Mercy hoots.

"Yes," I whisper back. "Attempt to do better than the last one."

"I don't think people say that kind of thing to kings."

"If they had, maybe he wouldn't have raised a Jendaya and we wouldn't be in this mess."

He clicks his tongue irritably and I glance at his troubled face. For a king – even one who does not reign, for in Cragspear the direct descendant reigns and Stekkan is nothing more than a pretty prize to bring out at balls and state occasions – he seems very angry.

"*And so, he should be. His future has been stolen and who knows what else.*"

Vargaard is warming to our new king.

"*It's not me who has changed. It's him.*"

I'd like to press him on that, but suddenly all five of the swords below are drawn and I see Nakuraki leap forth in their shadows. It's too far away to make out details but I hold my breath and it feels like Vargaard is holding his breath, too.

I try to examine them. Even breathing feels dangerous. They'll see me up here. They will come for my soul. And Vargaard is good, but is he good enough to fend off five more of his kind?

*"No. Though it pains me to admit, I would not be sufficient against them, Vali."*

Jendaya turns behind her and gives an order and then six soldiers march forward with a large iron box on their shoulders that is carried on a pair of poles. The soldiers walk behind and before with the poles held over their shoulders and when they are in front of Jendaya, they slowly lower the box and step aside.

She places the green gem in the center of the box.

*"Oh no."*

Oh no, what? Vargaard?

But my shadow seems frozen.

"Loyal friends," Jendaya says. "It is time to reform the world into what it will be. It is time to bring all mortals to the next level of our powers and the potential of our souls. Only the strongest can survive what comes next. I will be among them as your Queen, but will you be brave enough to claim what is yours?"

"You'd think that as king I could stop her from whatever she's doing," Stekkan says, frustrated.

"I think you shouldn't count on that," I whisper.

"The time of the weak and the time of the soft has passed,"

Jendaya says. "The time of holding us back, the time of shouting about distinctions and individuality has gone with it. Together, we will build something new, and none shall stand in our way."

The traitor nobles representing their countries murmur agreement, and then, one by one, they take turns standing before Jendaya and bowing over her hand – the sign of one monarch acknowledging the next.

I see the Calla Magna's tinkling ruby earrings sway as she bends and as she moves aside, the swishing robes of the Hexipluris take her place.

"This can't be happening," Stekkan whispers. "Who do we have left to stop them all? They've gone mad. They'll destroy the world."

"My father," the words are out before I can stop them.

"And what will he do?" Stekkan asks, turning his hopeless gaze on me as if he thinks I might fill the empty space behind his eyes where hope used to be.

And I don't know why I feel sure, but I do. I feel like somehow he'll know what to do. That he'll know where to go. That if we can't escape by land, mayhap we can escape by sea. But I have no reasoning behind my hopes.

"I don't know," I say. "But I'm not giving up."

"And I'm not leaving you," Stekkan says, jaw firming. "I vowed to stick with you, monster hunter. And while I can no longer offer you the privileges or comforts of a marriage to a duke, I can at least offer you what I do have."

"Musical talent?" I ask lightly, trying not to be ill as I see Count Lansdown cut a finger and then jam his blade into a slot on the iron box beside the gem.

I don't know which blade it is, but it's shaped like the Mercy Sword only made from some kind of metal that looks nearly white in the morning sun.

"A kingly taste in fashion," Stekkan says with mock seriousness. "And an ability to patch up wounds. Both of which seem to fill gaps in your own abilities, oh hunter of monsters."

I chuckle. I'm about to watch the world end, I realize. I can't stop it. I can only watch. But at least I have a good friend and the shadow I love to watch it end along with me. Together, we can be contented for the last moments of the world.

"*Love,*" Vargaard echoes in his baritone mental voice and it sounds like a purr of contentment.

Always. I think I will always love him now that I've started. Even if always ends up being very, very short.

"*I do not think I could bear to lose this so soon after finding it. And yet, Ilsaletta, I have a confession.*"

Another confession. He seems to have a wealth of those.

"*This one is new. I fear it may be my duty to stop my brethren of the sword.*"

I don't know what that means.

"*The Nakuraki.*"

Well, of course we'll stop them. If we can. If we see a way.

"*Without you.*"

How can it be without me when he's in my shadow? It's not even a thing that's possible.

I feel him shift like he wants to answer, but before he can, the last sword is slotted in place and Jendaya draws a blade of her own – a tiny thing the size of my palm – and brings it down hard into the Duchess's back.

I'd forgotten Stekkan's aunt was even there. She's still kneeling, choking on her own blood as the watchmen and guard who were with her strain against a greater force, bellowing their despair.

Jendaya, cool as a long night in winter, kicks her over onto the gem where she spasms, coughing blood.

"This with blood, we are sealed," Jendaya declares, loud enough to fill the square even over the gasping protests of the men I spent all night fighting beside. They're as helpless as we are – as useless as we are – in the face of this continued nightmare.

With her declaration, something tears.

At first, I think it's inside me, but then I realize the whole of the earth is shuddering under our feet, the stone tower swaying in a way that a built thing never should. Stekkan stumbles back, stricken with grief. We clutch at each other for support, our eyes meeting in shared horror before turning down to the square where something like a rip in cloth is forming in the very air. Where it rips, it cuts everything in twain. A tree tumbles from the edge of the square, the top cloven from the bottom, a tall building of stone follows it. To the other side, people are ripped apart as easily as cows are halved by a competent butcher. And then the gap bulges and wrenches apart and the earth shudders again as the air and ground gather and pull apart like fabric. And from the open wound in the fabric of reality, smoke and shadows claw their way out.

The first to spill through the womb of hell is a three-headed panther like the ones we fought, but hard on its heels is a wave of roiling shadow bodies as if someone has broken a dam and the

Sea of Souls is about to wash out onto the land.

*"That is exactly what you are seeing."*

And I don't need Vargaard to tell me, but he still does.

*"Run."*

# Chapter Twenty-Six

I don't run right away. Instead, I drop Stekkan's arm, and I hurry to the black flag, hauling on the rope to lift it.

*"No time. No time."*

I've never heard Vargaard sound like this before. It's worse than the ground shaking. Worse than watching the world rip open and souls spill out. It's like watching a mountain fall over in front of your eyes, like losing your legs. I don't know what to do with how it makes me feel, so I concentrate on the prickly jute rope, and I pull.

I am the feather. I float over this world. I am the feather.

The wind snaps the flag over me, filling it like a sail and snapping my long black hair out behind my head to match it. It's like I'm setting out upon the sea, and I wish I was. I wish I could sail off into the horizon and chase the sun from east to west and never see another person again.

There's a muffled sob and I spare a glance for Stekkan. His hand is over his mouth, his eyes so wide they fill his face.

He's watching the ground below and then he spins to look at me and with his voice shaking harder than the ground did, he drops his hand and says, "Hell has opened up its mouth to eat us."

*"Eat us,"* Mercy agrees from his shoulder.

"What should we do?" he asks me and how should I know? I'm Ilsaletta Redtide. I like books and maps. I like to daydream I'm leading the Charge of the Black Brassars but really, I just take long walks on the sand without my boots on. How should I know what to do?

*"I've got you,"* Vargaard seems to be back to normal. Maybe. I'm still worried about him. First talk of leaving me and then that panic. But his mental voice is the same – like the purr of a lion. *"You can trust me."*

I take a deep breath and remember the Mercy Sword is not the only weapon we have here.

"We make our stand," I say and I am the feather, I float above the earth. I am not the girl with the trembling hands and stinging eyes. I'm the feather.

*"I would not recommend it. This is a very defensible position. Which will mean our deaths will be long and drawn out as we hack them back for hours only to be slowly overwhelmed."*

I can see that in my mind's eye, and for a moment I'm ill with fear. But then I am the feather, and that, too, fades.

And what is wrong with Vargaard. He isn't like this. He's always confident, always certain.

*"It's my brothers who opened that tear – the other Nakuraki. It is they who fight against us."*

Well, that's been true since Jendaya used one of them to put us in Stekkan's glass pendant.

*"But that was just one. This is all of them — all but she who sleeps in Stekkan's sword."*

That makes the odds worse, but it doesn't change the substance of what's happening.

I can hear them on the stairs now. I can hear them rushing to fill the cathedral. I'm trying so hard to be the feather, but the edges of my calm are fraying.

*"They're my responsibility. I share their guilt."*

I pause. Is Vargaard having a dark night of the soul right now? When true monsters are climbing up the stairs? Is he being plagued by misplaced guilt when we're about to be butchered like animals?

You are, aren't you?

He's silent for a long moment.

Divine Sovereign! He's having a crisis of conscience and taking all this on himself right now when we're about to be overrun by monsters and souls.

*"Farrakki,"* Vargaard says. *"That's what they are named in the legends — strange creatures made by the nightmares of men."*

I lick my lips, positioning myself just out of view of the trapdoor. It's far too late to run from farrakki or anything else.

Stekkan bravely stands behind me.

We'll face this together. Sort of. I can't help but worry for the city guard and the soldiers we fought alongside through the night. They were down in that square when the farrakki poured through the tear. Will any of them survive that first wave?

I left them alone to die. I'd thought they were safe. I'd thought *we* were the ones taking the risk.

*"I have failed you. I cannot stop the farrakki. I cannot fight them off for long. I cannot keep hell from hunting you down and swallowing your soul."*

And I could not keep them from destroying my allies from just hours ago. None of us could fix this or save the rest. Maybe no one ever could. Maybe it was always going to happen like this. Worrying about it won't fix anything now, it will just spoil our last moments with the taste of guilt.

I need to be watching for the first one of them to pop his head through the trap door, not fussing over who is dying because of whom.

But his words have distracted me.

Instead, I turn so I can see his flickering face. Vargaard?

*"Yes."*

"I need you." It's strange how hard it is to make this confession when it's so obvious.

"I'll be here," Stekkan says tightly, thinking I'm talking to him and that's fine. He needs reassurance, too.

*"I will never leave you."*

And that is all that I ask of him. Just not to leave me. Just to hold my hand with his shadowed one as I die. I've never asked for more and I'm not about to start.

He seems to melt at my words and then he's right there, cupping my face in his shadowed hand and I swear I can see a dark tear trickle down his face.

*"You deserve so much more."*

I have so much more than I deserve.

*"I would give you the world if I could."*

He's already given me more than I knew was possible.

I feel his shadowed lips on mine for the barest moment as his kiss turns violent enough to make him corporeal. I cling to that whisper touch leaning toward it so that I almost stumble forward when it melts into tender kindness.

*"To my last breath,"* he vows, falling to one knee, eyes still on mine.

And to mine.

Forever.

I hear the squeak of the stair below the trap door.

"I saw something," Stekkan whispers and I realize his breathing isn't right. He's going to faint if he does that. "Something in your shadow. It looked like a man. Oh, seas and stars. It … it bowed on one knee like a knight."

His breath whistles sharply.

"Stekkan," I say as calmly as I can.

"Yes?" he squeaks.

"Draw your sword."

I hear it rasp in his fumbling hands as the first head peeks up through the trap door. I stab it in the eye.

# CHAPTER TWENTY-SEVEN

They pour up the stairs like a flood and my Vargaard is fast
– so fast – but no one can be fast enough for this. We whirl and
strike, duck and weave, and we are driven back inch by inch.
Bodies pile around us – two, three, four deep – shadow bodies
of the farraki and much more gory bodies of half-humans with
smoke pouring from their fractured skulls or full humans with
smoke ringing them.

I duck one blow only to be slammed in the side by another.
And then slammed again when I recover enough to stand.

Vargaard cries out beside me, and it rips something inside me.
Can hearts bleed while you still live?

Mine is bleeding. I taste blood in my mouth and on my lips.
I'm pressed backward, backward, hair flapping wildly in the
wind, Vargaard flapping wildly in my shadow as his workman-
like blows fall precisely where he puts them. We are killing and
injuring and we're also falling back. There are too many. All I see
when I look is the press of one cluster of smoke and spirit against
the next.

Something strikes me hard and my leg crumples under me.

I fall to the ground, try to get up, and fall again. My injured leg won't take the weight. A Farrakki leaps from the pack and sinks its teeth into my shoulder and I don't know if it's a panther or a wolf or something between the two, only that it's terrifying and dark and I'm overwhelmed.

A gasp tears from me, and then suddenly he's there, standing over me, hunched, taking the blows meant for me. They shred his shadows and claw at his edges, and he tears and shreds and still he stands.

And I'm losing him. I'm feeling his gritted teeth and determination, but I'm also feeling that I'm losing him a fluttering scrap at a time and I'm not ready.

Not like this.

Not for me.

I love him too much.

"To. My. Last." He is saying and his words are growing fainter and I reach for him to pull him against me, but my hands just go through him. I choke on these words, and I know that when he goes, I won't be far behind and it's my only comfort.

A hand grabs my good ankle and starts to pull and I'm slipping out from under him. A sob tears through my chest. Not because I'm scared, but because I'm losing him. I catch his eye and he smiles, and I think he's trying to say something but it's not coming.

"My sun."

And then he's a burst of black smoke and then he's nothing at all.

I'm choking. I'm dying. I slash out wildly with my sword, catching a mostly human monster with the edge. They part for a breath and in that breath, I catch a glimpse of the entire bell tower. It's full of writhing monsters. One of them grabs the bell pull and the huge brass bell clangs a single deafening clatter.

*Clang.*

Something digs painfully into my thigh and hands grab my sword hand, trying to rip the Mercy Sword free.

*Clang.*

Not. That.

I clench my teeth and hold it tighter, both hands wrapped around the blade. And I don't understand how this happened so fast.

*Clang.*

This is death, I'm trying to tell myself. No one expects it to come so quickly. It just does. Make your peace with it.

I'm losing my grip and then pain flares so hard in my leg that I can't take the agony. I scream and scream and there's nothing but me and the Mercy Sword and the scream going on forever.

*Cl-ang.*

*Clang.*

*Cl-ang.*

*Clang.*

I'll die to the deafening sound of a bell. The thought makes me want to laugh but between the bell peals and my wild screams and the dark forms blocking out the morning sun, towering over me and around me like a forest of mushrooms suddenly springing up from the rot of what had once been my dreams, I think I hear the whisper of, *"Mercy."*

I feel a touch unlike the rest on my uninjured shoulder and as I spin to look, I know I'm dreaming, because a very calm Stekkan leans over me, somehow utterly unseen by the monsters surrounding us and he puts his glass pendant around my neck, and everything goes black.

# NAKURAKI

I am plunged into the Sea of Souls, battered and trampled by the denizens here and it's all I can do to pull myself to my feet. In this place, knowing who you are is essential. It keeps you from shattering, keeps you strong. But the weight of my failure presses down on me.

First, my kind turned to evil – again. At the hands of a monster of a human – again. With nothing I could do to stop it. Something tries to catch my attention at that thought, but all I smell is rot.

Second, my failure to her, my sun and stars. I promised her I would defend her. Promised her she would be safe with me and in her moment of trial I buckled, my courage failed, and it took her words to pull me from the brink. Words she shouldn't have had to speak. Words that *I* should have spoken to *her*.

The weight of it grinds me down and I do not care that I am trampled under the feet of souls more confident, more buoyant than I. I shall sink into the sea and so be it. I deserve no less.

I will rot like the other Vargaards in the back of my mind – rot and fade and remain nothing more than a memory that cannot be grasped and how can I protest that when it is only just.

From the edge of my vision, I catch a glimpse of a soul dressed in the harness of the Akul Khanani priests. His harness bears two pairs of crossed swords. Strange that I still remember the garb of the Akul Khanani when I cannot remember ever meeting one. And then he's gone again. Just an illusion brought to me in my delirium.

I don't dare let myself fall entirely. I don't dare surrender to the loneness. I have to stay close to this place for I am certain she will join me soon. For I failed in that, too. I failed to protect her body, my shadow-self torn to pieces like wool is sheared from a sheep. And I will stay in this place grimly waiting until she joins me so that I can do her one last service and take her to the other side before I leave her.

I have no place at her side. Not now that I have failed her.

But I can at least do this one funeral rite.

A glimmer in the sea above and I catch a glimpse of the Fisher King. He lets his net down, golden and flashing, waiting to harness one blessed soul and bear him to the lands beyond – the promised lands where loved ones await, and endless rest has come.

I ignore the net. It is not here for me. Perhaps one day. Perhaps, in time.

And then – fast as a fish darting to catch the bait – the net has caught me, and I'm being dragged upward.

VARGAARD. The word is an echo in my mind. Inaudible. Undeniable. COME HOME, FAITHFUL.

Faithful? Surely, he cannot mean my ragged soul, the rotting mass of Vargaards that were and the new, fresh broken Vargaard that is now. There has been a mistake.

Every eye is on me as the sea writhes and grasps. Every heart wants to be where I am.

THERE IS NO MISTAKE.

I am filled with unwarranted hope. With a sense of wondrous humility. It is not right that I have been chosen. Not right, and yet I have wanted nothing more. And all I would have to do to claim this golden fate is to surrender to it. Peace steals over me, binding my wounds, leeching into my thoughts. I let it wash me, cleanse me, settling into the cracks and grooves worn into my aching heart.

All I have to do is surrender.

I look up wistfully at the Fisher King and I know that somewhere beyond him my mother and sisters await. Somewhere beyond him are Valis of the past. Friends, perhaps. And all I need to do to reach them is nothing at all. I could seek their forgiveness. I could find real peace. It can all be mine. And I want it so badly that tears are forming, sobs of relief welling up in my chest.

But at the same time, something within my heart is tearing. I snatch at it, trying to breathe, feeling my fluttering breaths caught in my ragged throat.

The hope – silken and beguiling – is lost, fluttering away in tattered ash.

This is not for me. It cannot be for me. Not without Ilsaletta. My sun. My stars. I cannot leave her in this morass of souls, alone and unguarded. If she is left to suffer here then I will suffer with her.

"Please," I beg. "Not without her. Please."

My plea is heard.

I'm released and falling, falling as the golden net drags upward without me. A fish tossed back to the sea.

I land in the morass of souls, the impact jarring me hard. I'm trembling, shaking right through with what I've done, my lip trembling, my heart trembling with it. The peace – so powerful moments before – is gone like mist in the sun.

And then she is beside me so suddenly that I almost startle, but unlike all others, she is motionless, falling between heedless feet and trampled under them without raising a hand in her own defense.

This is why I chose. My heart grows firm.

Horrified, I shove and batter at the souls around me until I can sink beside her and clasp her to my breast, and I don't care that I'm sobbing. I don't care about the hollow sounds shuddering me apart. I don't care that my blurred vision is throwing up foolish fantasies – visions of other Nakuraki riding on the backs of farrakki, whips cracking over the heads of the souls of men as they drive them forward in apocalyptic return. I feel the hairs of my body stand on end and something within my spirit rises at the sight, called to join them despite my new loyalties. There, in the shadows behind them, I see the priest of the blades again and his head tilts to the side, his eyes narrowing as he watches me as if I am the one thing in his universe that stands out. I know – somehow – that I'm seeing something I need to remember, that I'm seeing the key to all of this, but I can't seem to care.

She is the sun. The stars. The beauty of the vast black sky. And this is not the place for the sparkle of the Divine eye to find herself.

With a roar, I find my feet, bearing her up in my arms, the

fibers of my muscles all twisting to one purpose. Her clothing is tattered. Her black hair streams around us as her head hangs limply, dangling. And yet I cling to her as if she is my still salvation, as if she is lifting me. Because she is.

And then my vision goes double and for a terrible moment, I see two things at once. I see the Seas of Souls writhing around us and flowing in a way it never flows – toward the unnatural rent in the fabric of reality and freedom, I would guess – and I see a hand reach for the Mercy Sword and pick it up. I must still have some kind of attachment to that sword to see the new bearer of it.

Wait.

Terror streaks through me like rancid oil, turning my bile and heart to dust. What if in her death I do not go with her? What if I am bound back to the sword?

My heart is thundering.

What if it drags me away and I am forced to leave her here?

And now I can hardly bear it. I kiss her fading cheek, her soft rose lips, her slender throat.

Pause.

There is a pulse there. Here in this spirit world, it's false of course. We aren't physical here. And yet, I feel it. She lives.

Hope hurts like a blade in the belly.

The hand holding the Mercy Sword moves and I realize the owner clutches two swords. The Mercy Sword and the Tranquility Sword and I fall into his shadow while still being trapped in the Sea of Souls. A green glass pendant swings against the bare flesh of his chest and I realize without knowing how I realize it, that

Stekkan has put Ilsaletta back in his pendant.

He strides with deep calm, slowly easing himself around one terrifying nightmare after another, refusing to look away from the sword in his hand, not when a man is butchered beside him, viscera splashing across Stekkan's pretty jacket. Not when a woman pleads for help just two paces away as her skull cracks and white smoke pours out. Not as his bird shrieks and moans and wails upon his shoulder.

"Mercy, mercy, mercy," it cries and my bitter soul cries with it, one in this moment of elongated agony.

But the duke, or perhaps the prince, but now the king, he walks steadily, calmly onward and not a single nightmare sees him, or stops him.

And I clutch my beloved Ilsaletta and count her heartbeats and my breath hangs in the air as I realize that all our fates – all three of us, my sun, the crazed bird, and me – rest on the shoulders of a man who is shaking as the last leaf of a tree in a high wind of autumn, that slowly he is crying – like the sides of a weeping jug on a warm day – as he eases us mile after mile through a landscape of hell and out of the vast city of Swordheart and through the open gates.

And I don't know if he can hear me, but I speak calming words to him and I find the calm words are working on me, too.

"You can do this, Stekkan Falrune, King of Cragspear," I whisper and my mouth is dry as I try to channel into him the confidence I would give a new recruit on the eve of his first battle. My heart aches at the consolation of peace I thrust away from myself when I turned my back on the Fisher King's offer. But it aches, too, with this hope. "Take heart. Take courage. Find within you the man of honor and be that man. You have not failed – not yet – if only you can keep your courage close."

We walk on and on.

And to my utter shock, I am crying with him, tear for tear, and when he falls to the ground weeping on a hill outside the city, many hours later, dropping both swords at his feet, I am weeping, too.

And when – at last – he slashes his palm and smears it over the glass bauble, I hold my breath and I hold my hope just as he holds my future, and the world goes dark.

When I open my eyes again, I am nothing but a shadow. And I've never felt so grateful to be only a whisper of a man. I've never felt such roaring gratitude at my own damnation. For my sun is whole and alive and lying in the grass at my feet as her king helps her sit and asks gently if she is whole.

My life for hers. My future for hers.

Always.

And I bow my head, hold my breath, and bite my lip, just as worried as he is, until her eyes – frantic – find mine. In them, are all the waters of the endless sea and she says with a smile, "I am whole as long as I have my shadow."

And I am whole for as long as I have my sun.


***


*Read more of Ilsaletta and Vargaard's Story in "Seas of Shadow."*

# BEHIND THE SCENES:

USA Today bestselling author, Sarah K. L. Wilson loves happy endings, stories that push things just a little further than you expect, heroes who actually act heroic, selfless acts of bravery, and second chances. She writes young adult fantasy because fantasy is her home and apparently her internal monologue is stuck in the late teens

Sarah would like to thank **Melissa Wright & Eugenia Kollia** for their incredible work in beta reading and proofreading this book. Without their big hearts and passion for stories, this book would not be the same.

Sarah has the deepest regard for the talent of her phenomenal artist Luciano Fleitas who created the gorgeous cover art that accompanies this book. Without his work, it would be so much harder to show off this story the way it deserves!

Thanks also to the Noble Order of Female Fantasy Authors who keep me sane – sort of. And for my beloved husband, Cale and sons Neville and Leif who are endlessly patient as I talk to them about bookish passions.

And a HUGE THANK YOU to my patrons, **Mike Burgess, Jennifer Wood,** and **Carly Salsbury** for their support. I couldn't do this without readers like you!

Visit Sarah's website for more information:

www.sarahklwilson.com